Aaron Ramos

THE

GARDEN

and other stories

Cover design by: Henry Wong

ISBN: 9798643497936

Dedicated to my daughter Sakura.
You caused such a delay to the writing of these stories
that I thought I'd never finish any of them,
but without you they wouldn't exist.

CONTENTS

PREFACE

This book is the first collection of my work all in one place. Up until now my stories have only been read by close friends and family, and I'd like to thank every one of them for their help in this endeavour. I am both excited and daunted to introduce it to the world and possibly the universe at large, and whatever else that may entail as a result.

Please enjoy the book, ask yourself big questions and take comfort in the fact that we all share many of the same thoughts, emotions and feelings. Below is a quote I wanted to include that sums up beautifully the feelings and ideas I try to evoke as people read my stories.

"Let's suppose that you were able every night to dream any dream that you wanted to dream. And that you could, for example, have the power within one night to dream seventy-five years of time. Or any length of time you wanted to have. And you would, naturally as you began on this adventure of dreams, you would fulfil all your wishes. You would have every kind of pleasure you could conceive. And after several nights of seventy-five years of total pleasure each, you would say, "Well, that was pretty great." But now let's have a surprise. Let's have a dream which isn't under control. Where something is gonna happen to me that I don't know what it's going to be. And you would dig that and come out of that and say, "Wow, that was a close shave, wasn't it?" And then you would get more and more adventurous, and you would make further and further out gambles as to what you would dream. And finally, you would dream… where you are now. You would dream the dream of living the life that you are actually living today."

- Alan Watts

VIDEO GAME THEORY

There should be a word for that feeling you get when you notice the passing of time. When you're older, I hope you want to play video games like me. Telling you this won't affect whether you do or you don't, but I want to feel like I'm giving you something now that I'm gone. When I was a kid, the first video game I ever completed was *Disney's Aladdin* on the *Commodore Amiga*. My mother bought that hulking pixelated monstrosity for digital design and animation in a time before she could afford photoshop. We never had much money growing up. You've probably never seen one before.

She's an illustrator by trade, and trained at the Los Angeles college of design. You know she told me that once, to pass an exam at school, she had to draw a perfect circle freehand! Can you imagine? My childhood was filled with her elaborate drawings and delicate paintings. I remember grizzled wart-covered goblins and awkward gangly trolls, children and their dragons, and caves to put them in. Her teacher was Chuck Jones, the creator of *Loony Toons*. *Road Runner* and *Speedy Gonzalez* were my favourites. I always thought the ability to run that fast would be the greatest super power imaginable. You could leave clouds of smoke behind you and escape anyone that would ever want to hurt you. I think I'm going that fast now. I'm getting further away, and I want to teach you the six things playing games taught me, before I'm too far for this message to reach you.

My mother is also a massive nerd just like I am. I bet you will be too. She was the one that introduced me to both *Hobbits* and *Star Wars*. When I was young, I would take two striped cushioned chairs we had in the living room and put them on their sides end to end to make a fort by the big living room window. The same living room window that I can swear to you I saw the Easter bunny through one year. You should ask your grandmother, she won't even say I imagined it. We had an old red bean bag that I would throw inside the two chairs before clambering in and curling up with *The Lord of the Rings*. Books were my other escape from the cruel echoing voices of my schoolmates, and the harshness of the urban sprawl that we lived in.

My imagination was nourished daily like the plants she loved in our small back garden. A rare patch of lush green surrounded by miserable grey and muck stained white. She and your grandfather were happy once, and together they built a tall wooden climbing frame there for your uncle and I. Our names were written in the cement that held each wooden pole into the earth and rich clay. I miss the sensations of solid ground under my feet.

The view is spectacular from up here though, I hope the pictures made it to you.

If I ever needed something to do, my mother encouraged me to read and write and draw and create for creations sake. My upbringing was littered like our living room with waxy coloured crayons and pencils, and papers of every thickness and colour. I learned what the force of creativity is, and that when you *make something,* everything like that connects to everything else. She played the guitar as well, and sang. She sang all the time and filled our home with music, just like your mama. All these things I've tried my hand at over the years too, thanks to her.

It's lonely out here, but that's to be expected. I hope you feel like your mama and I support you in everything that you do. I've never had a supporter quite like your grandmother. Well, that is, until I met your mama. When I told her my plans to man *the Gödel* and fly out as a volunteer, I knew she didn't want me to, but she made me go anyway. That's the thing about being an adult, you won't always see eye-to-eye on everything or even believe the same things. The secret that most people don't know is that you can live with and love each other anyway. In fact the best ones are the ones you disagree with the most. You'll probably hate me for leaving at first, but in time I hope you understand why.

I want you to grow up creative like my mother, and strong like yours. I bet you're athletic, like your mama. I remember sports day on a sweaty summertime afternoon. The ground was littered everywhere with the pink and white spring blossoms in huge hilly piles all over the ground, and wedged into the corners of red brick walls. Whenever it was hot the playground at school would cook and fill your nose with a chemical asphalt fragrance. There was a novelty race, where the boys had to dress in their mother's clothing and run a hundred metres. Would you believe your grandmother used to wear tracksuits and running shoes? You'd never guess looking at her now. It was the only race I won in my life.

Isn't it funny that I'm trying to teach you with a message from the future, but that ultimately I can't change a thing? I wonder if I'll be remembered by anyone, or if I'll just be a blip in history. A footnote. I think ultimately my life will be defined by the strong women that were part of it. No matter what it is I set out to do, they are both there by the sidelines, cheering me on with their whole hearts. I'm so lucky that we made you so I have another strong woman to cherish. Sometimes I feel bad that I'm not the best at showing it. I should have called my mother more.

By the time you are able to read this, you'll probably wonder why I was so selfish and left. I couldn't give you all the reasons, and to say it was completely for the good of mankind would be a lie. Some of it was for me. It had to be. I hope you're the kind of woman that makes up her own mind. How could you not be?

I always fancied being the hero, ever since *Star Wars*. I didn't want to be Skywalker though, I always preferred *Han Solo*. There was something about that devil-may-care attitude that always appealed to me. All he needed was a sarcastic comeback and his trusty blaster to get the job done. I'm not really like him in the least though, life isn't that simple. I guess what I'm trying to say here is that I'm sorry, and that it's ok to be a mess sometimes. Sorry that you grew up without me. I want you to read this and know that I didn't leave because of you. You need to hear it from me and no one else.

By leaving on *the Gödel*, I'll be able to contribute in some small way to securing a future where you can still go outside. You will have read by now what our mission was, where I am now. The timeline of it all really messes with my head. It will take me and the crew eighteen years to reach *Salutis Major,* and another eighteen years for reports of our success to reach Earth again. In that time we'll have set up the colony. We'll be ready and waiting with open arms to ferry half of humanity out here, and save that beautiful blue and green ball we all love from the environmental doom we were too short sighted to set right in time.

So now sacrifices like those being made by *the Gödel* and her crew are necessary. I'm sorry it means I won't be able to see you at any age but this one. The further I get from earth, the weaker the signal will be until eventually I won't be able to send anything. It might be confusing to you at first, but as you get older this message will start to make sense. I just hope you can forgive me.

Your grandmother also introduced me to video games on that *Commodore Amiga*. We grew up in a rough area in south east London, England. Screaming and sirens were the melody at all times of the day. Fighting between enemies and families, shootings and stabbings, midnight drug raids and dog attacks were a weekly occurrence. I used to resent her for not letting me play outside with some of the neighbourhood kids but now looking back, I think I realise why. Even if she'd wanted to protect me from the choices I made that led me here, she couldn't have. That's ironic too I suppose.

My mother used to let me play games as soon as I got home *first,* before I had to do any homework. I'm not sure she realised anything about the order that things took place, but I've taken it to heart. It's going to take me a lot to persuade your mama to let me do the same for you but I'm going to try. They taught me a lot. I'd get home around four pm, sprint up the stairs on all fours to the back room which doubled as both junk and computer den, and smelled like mould. I could play games till around five pm, then i'd do my homework after, and then play some more, or with my toys till dinner. During and after dinner the whole family would gather round the cool blue glow of the television, and watch movies or our weekly shows together snuggled up on the sofa under blankets until bed time. I remember wolfing down huge helpings of tomato pasta with browned beef mince and crisped cheddar cheese on top. What I wouldn't give for some real cheese right now.

I want you to know that unless you *love* your job, I think the idea of taking your work home with you is outrageous. You know I used to work in an office once? I hated it. Every five minutes I used to think about jumping out the window. Not to die mind you, but to see if I could just fly away. I guess I managed it in the end. Remember I told you I have a very vivid imagination. I would feel held captive by the pearl buttons on my shirts that glinted like faint stars. It felt as if my silk ties were choking me. Trust me, everyone in an office is replaceable, that's one thing I learned over the years. Sooner or later robots are going to do everything anyway so it's better if you learn how to play as soon as you can, and do it as much as you can.

To actually go back and forth through time is impossible as you know, we're just using the incredible power of the temporal propulsion engine to make it outside the Milky Way. The thing about interstellar flight on a ship like *the Gödel* is that because of the speeds we travel at, myself and the crew experience time outside of it as a continual loop. Time passes normally for us inside, but in order to move so quickly it's distorted all around us. Torn and shredded temporarily as we carve our way through. The whole ship looks like it's sealed within a soap bubble. You'll read about it someday.

You're smart. I know it because I've seen it in your eyes. Those deep burnt chocolate brown eyes your mama gave you. You know at first I was sad they weren't grey-blue like mine? But then you looked at me for the first time. I remember looking into them when you were born and seeing nothing but potential. They glittered, completely unknowing but somehow knowing. You were everything there was and nothing all at once. Everything you could come to be was there, at the same time as nothing at all. It was like staring deep into the universe and speaking softly, waiting for an echo to come back in the unending silence. I could stare into those eyes for hours.

All I can do from here is send messages in a bottle, back to the exact same point I left you. All you'll ever have to me are two perfect opal teeth and that beautiful wispy hair dancing all over your head like cotton candy. Even though it's been years since I left, my words will reach you and your mama at the exact same second every single time. I can't teach you anything new or pass anything on, but I want to feel like I am. I want you to know how much I love you.

I never told my mother how grateful I was for teaching me that clear divide between school and home. You know if you let it, life can be one endless cycle of simply *getting by*. Don't let that happen to you. There was nothing worse for me as a kid than being at those dreary schools all day long, away from my family and home and comfort, surrounded by people who would never love me. I would write fake sick notes every week by typing them up and secretly printing them out, then forging my father's signature just to escape. It was easy to do, his handwriting looks like a spider dipped its feet in ink and ran across the page.

Aladdin actually took me years to complete. It's not like games nowadays where you can save your progress and come back to it later. That's a luxury you don't even realise you have. There are so many of those. Clean breathable air, even fresh water for that matter. Every time you restart on a new day, you have to begin again, and if you use up all your lives trying to pass a particular level, you have to restart from the very beginning. There was one stage that I hated and loved the most. It was based on the scene where the hero needs to escape from the Cave of Wonders after it's erupted into molten lava. You'll see the film one day I'm sure, your mama loves them. The music used to make my little heart beat faster as I'd grip the shiny black joystick and prepare to give it my best.

Again and again I relentlessly pushed those blue floppy disks into the drive, listening to the dull mechanical click as they went in with anticipation. After so many tries eventually I could speed play it. It was a loop in itself. Because I'd been there countless times my hands knew the movements perfectly as if I was synchronised with each byte of information before my eyes. I was one with the machine and I knew every detail about every level intimately. As an adult, this has helped not only my hand and eye coordination greatly, but my ability to problem solve and to fail with grace and dignity. I learned then that to become an expert, to be truly great at something, you have to immerse yourself in it. When you fail over and over, understand that you are simply learning something. And when you do finally master something, it's only just the beginning. It starts all over again.

One day, standing up from my chair with a triumphant roar in my lungs, I did it. I completed the whole thing from start to finish. I do that often in the morning you know. I get out of bed and just shout. If you asked me why I couldn't tell you. There should be a word for that too. The screen went dark and seven words appeared in the black that remained.

Well done.
Press any button to start.

ELEVATED

She ate with her hands on the first date. Marcus wasn't used to someone so new in his life being so utterly comfortable in their own skin. It gave him pangs of anxiety as Riley picked up bundles of french fries dipped delicately into a minuscule amount of sauce, each greasy mouthful after the next. Despite himself, he smiled. Her comfort was contagious.

"What?"

"Nothing." Marcus somehow couldn't keep the corners of his mouth in check and carefully wiped the sauce from his lips with a neatly folded napkin. Hers lay in a crinkled mess on the table and he wanted to fold it too. *How can someone so small possibly store all that food inside such a tiny frame?* He wondered.

"You're smirking…"

"What? No, it's nothing. It's just…you're making me hungry and I've almost finished my food." She stared, chewing slowly, and smiled, mouth still full and greasy full lips glistening in the pink neon lights of the tiny restaurant.

Their meeting was unconventional by societal standards, and Marcus considered so too. Ever since the introduction of automated artificial intelligence systems to the city of London, most people looking for love simply trusted in *the algorithm*. Matches were said to be somewhere in the range of eighty-nine to ninety-four percent perfect. With that kind of success rate, no one really dared argue against the aggressively clinical approach.

Marcus had both marvelled at and abhorred how artificial intelligence had almost completely replaced working class human beings in all areas of every day life. The general consensus was agreed upon almost universally. Why trust a human, when a highly sophisticated and relatively cheap machine could execute the job more perfectly than they could ever aspire to? The tendrils of AI ran all global transport systems, infected entertainment software, even job application sites. *The algorithm* knew what you wanted to do with your life better than you did. Most people liked it that way.

Marcus fiddled angrily with a few buttons on his home computer system that morning, as each smart suggestion was thrown at him one after the other for breakfast.

Why not try out the new imported American ZeroBagel! Only FIVE minutes from home on your morning journey to work. You'd be crazy not to grab one Marcus!

He ignored the ad, swiping it off screen with his index finger. He'd often choose exactly the opposite of what was suggested to him, and wondered if he bothered checking the screen each morning simply to make himself angry. There was something cathartically pointless to him about raging against the status quo, even if for no other reason than to declare to himself that he existed, that he mattered. He threw on his creased jacket and made his way out the door to the train station. These days you had to practically step over the displaced workers, vast throngs of the homeless gathered in a heaving stinking mass. The transition to automation hadn't been without its cost.

He watched the high-rise crystal towers loom across a grizzled and grey skyline, flicking by the train window and causing mosaics of light to dance on the seats and faces around him. All the clean air acts and micro-purifiers in Europe couldn't do anything about the murk that hovered over London. At ground level however, the city planners had done enough to fool everyone on their daily commutes into thinking things were far greener than they actually were. *Plant enough holographic trees and the illusion works pretty well.* Marcus mused.

His old Personal Communication Device (PCD) had been damaged for forty-eight hours the day his eyes met hers. It was common opinion among his close friends that he was the most easily distracted among them. His mind was a littered mess of half started projects that never amounted to anything other than disappointment and pent up anger. Watching his fellow passengers craning their necks into their screens on the morning commute, he found himself wondering what would happen if he ran down the carriage and knocked them all out of their hands.

Before PCD's people had melded seamlessly with their phones, and before phones, people had stuffed their faces into the daily newspapers. Business as usual, a fact the advertising companies were swift to jump on when in-floor advertising was first rolled out. Beautiful new carbon reinforced glass display floors set the city aglow all day, and made it especially disorienting at night. Marcus often stopped at high points overlooking the city in the evenings, just to enjoy the multicoloured star scape. He stared listlessly at the floor in the absence of anything better to do, a steady stream of booze, sexual performance stimulants and real estate ads streamed by under his feet.

He alighted the train close to his office, pushing through the heaving masses. He was not what you would call athletic, but enjoyed the stop-and-start dance of overtaking and cutting people off as he dashed through the transit tunnels. As he emerged into daylight he made for the nearest coffee outlet. The one he settled on had been a very old and very classic piece of British architecture once. Ornate stonework exterior and plaster moulding was now intermingled with plate display glass and sleek modern furniture.

He noticed her at first not just because he found her attractive, but because she wasn't carrying a

PCD. In fact she was looking up unlike everybody else, gazing around at the architecture of the room and generic modern art on the walls. He realised then if it wasn't for the fact his device was faulty, he never would have seen her at all. He didn't like the idea of fate as you couldn't control its outcome, even though the concept flickered around in his mind from time to time.

She was short in stature but athletic looking. *Maybe she was a sprinter in university?* He thought. Her hair was long, jet black and thick, tied up in a simple bun at the top of her head. *The sensible type.* She wore oversized black and white trainers and a simple grey tank top tucked loosely into comfortable, slim light blue jeans. No matter which way he looked at her, he couldn't place her ethnicity. She was definitely mixed, but he had no idea from where.

She caught him looking across the coffee shop. Their eyes met and a surge of decidedly awkward electricity streamed through Marcus' chest. He felt his skin tingle, and quickly averted his eyes to the server counter, obscuring his face by faking an itch. The AI servers made him uncomfortable at the best of times, and now all he could think of was that he had just been caught staring.

"Good morning sir, how do you like *your* coffee? Black as usual?" Said the glossy chrome humanoid shape in front of him in a perfectly well spoken, male British voice. The AI servers that interacted with the public were designed to look human, but only ever really came across as extremely sophisticated machines. They were convincing if you closed your eyes and ignored the streamlined outer chassis housing the AI units, but they lacked empathy. You couldn't relate to them and you couldn't forget you were talking to a computer. Marcus really didn't care for them. He had also never been to this coffee shop before and detested the assumption of his order.

"Uh…white, please, one sugar" Marcus replied nervously regretting it instantly. He hated white coffee.

"Sir my sensors are reading elevated sweat secretion levels coming from your body, might I suggest an iced frappe latte?" The AI was polite, but missing an important social cue as they so often did. Marcus was breathing faster now and his ears reddened.

"Just a white americano, please."

"Certainly sir," chirped the coffee server, "in addition, may I offer any snacks? A synth-protein cookie to compliment last night's workout? Or perhaps a dairy-substitute cheesecake due to your lactose intolerance? It's *my* personal favourite too."

Marcus was acutely aware there was no way this robot could have a favourite snack, they didn't consume anything solid but could process certain sugary liquids to substitute their fuel systems in a pinch. He knew it was just a program in the AI to make him at ease, but he wasn't feeling in the least bit relaxed by this point. He was often anxious and tense. It made him introverted and reclusive on his good days, and downright unreliable and absent on his bad ones.

He felt his face flush, the urge to leave was overwhelming. As the AI started to expound the virtues of the coffee house loyalty scheme, the small woman sidled up to him, leaning over his shoulder towards the coffee server with no regard for personal space.

"Just the white coffee for him please, and I'll take one of those protein cookies, yeah?" Marcus thought voice was extremely direct, commanding but somehow sweet. She made extended eye contact with the server, looking deep into its hollow, glowing sockets where the eyes should have been. Her hand was resting on its extended robotic limb. Before Marcus could react she whipped out her payment chip, paid the server for both items and then turned to face him, already chewing enthusiastically on her chocolate chip protein cookie. He looked down at the crumpled paper receipt she had pushed into his hand which read, *paid for by Riley.*

It was their third date and he didn't have any expectations, but he thought he'd try his luck anyway. Marcus finished his crisp lager beer, the alcohol had made him a more confident. *What's the worst that could happen?* The rain cascaded heavily outside, casting little rainbow reflections from the windows and the coloured lights inside the restaurant, mirroring the glass prism landscape of the city around them.

"So shall we…?" He started.

"What do you think about the weather system here in the city?" She asked abruptly. Riley looked at him seriously, waiting for a response. She clearly wasn't thinking what he was thinking.

"The weather system? The artificial one?" He offered, dejectedly picturing his sparsely decorated apartment waiting for his return.

"Yeah." Her demeanour had changed considerably, she looked at him seriously.

"Well, uh…it's like any other city weather system, right? We're shielded down here by the dome. Recycled air, recycled water, a whole system to give us a realistic portrayal of the *Great British* weather at this time of year." He didn't mask his sarcasm, he even felt slightly annoyed.

Marcus looked out at the rain bouncing off the glass walled city around them, fluorescent, and in technicolour. *Too realistic sometimes.* He thought miserably. He glanced upwards towards the sky. Even by straining his eyes he couldn't see behind the projected simulation rainclouds coming from the dome.

It was connected indirectly to a larger city AI system, commonly referred to as *The Mother*. He knew what lay beyond. Pollution, grime and filth, hovering endlessly above. *Now that I think of it, humanity really has done a number on the environment, here and everywhere else.* Why had he never given this more thought? Riley looked into the distance just past his head intently. "Do you ever wonder if it could be adapted though?"

"Adapted how?" All semblance of potential romance was dead to him. He resigned himself sullenly to the usual brush off he was accustomed to.

"Well, put the holograms aside. What does the city weather system do? It filters air and water, and pollution and waste, yeah? It also adds or subtracts heat to give us snow, or sunshine. Whatever they program, in an instant," the energy in her voice was electric. Marcus couldn't admit it right then but he was permeated by it. "The power requirements are enormous, but we manage with solar power because of the vast fields of panels *BetterTech* lobbied for before the dome first went up."

"Fuck *BetterTech.*" Marcus surprised himself with the outburst. Riley didn't blink.

"What do you mean?"

"My dad. He was a low-level tech support officer for them in the early days, before people like him were replaced with machines. He didn't realise it at first, but his own work made him obsolete."

"I'm sorry. I didn't know."

"Why would you? We just met." The same urge to run he had experienced at the coffee shop welled up as nausea within his stomach. "He had died a year after *The Mother* was up and running. The police report said it was a vehicle crash under the influence of alcohol and other stuff. *Reactionary depression* they called it." His voice cracked as he spoke and he grit his teeth tightly to keep himself under control. "The wreck was so bad that all that could be collected to identify him were his teeth. I was just a kid." He trailed off into silence, and began rummaging in his pockets for his payment card. It was time to go.

"*BetterTech* fucked it all up," she said softly. "You know, they were the ones that messed up the environment in the first place too, right?" She sounded irate to Marcus, he felt her trying to comfort him in her own way. He paid quickly before she could protest.

"Hey, shall I call you a car?" Riley's eyes flashed.

"I want to dance. Let's go, yeah?" That inflection at the end of her sentences. He found it annoyingly endearing. No sooner had the words left her lips, she was out the door, payment chip gliding across the counter, arms slipping into the sleeves of her simple leather jacket. It appeared both aggressive and graceful at once to Marcus.

Marcus could barely keep up as they arrived at the club Riley had chosen. It was a psychedelically lit multicoloured building in the style of a South American dive bar. Not his usual haunt if had a choice.

Intermingled with the human dancers were the AI servers and entertainers. Some took the shape of more graceful and sensual female forms, though decorated with beams of light and colour and with far more arms and legs than practically necessary. Others were part-machine part-holographic projection, casting obscenely intricate, rainbow fractal patterns and images across the sweating and thrusting forms of the club's patrons. The music was Latin-sounding, modern and easy to dance to, though dancing wasn't his thing in the least.

Marcus moved to the bar behind Riley as she slinked through the crowd, moving through so quickly towards the dance floor as to create slipstreams of bodies behind her. This was the first time they'd been anywhere like this, her energy was bewildering. As he ordered a beer he turned to ask her what she wanted, but Riley had torn off ahead, bursting onto the dance floor and diving among machine and skin alike.

She took the centre of the room as if that's where she belonged. Her body moved and blended with the crowd like she was blending with a larger entity, a smile spread wide across her face. Marcus felt a haze drift down over his eyes like a heavy curtain as he watched. He felt almost as if he were dizzy, but then only when he looked at her. She looked like a force of nature to him more than a person. He couldn't remember a time when he saw someone so free and so full of pure enjoyment. He felt as if his leads were lead as she broke away and drifted towards him grinning.

"Come and dance with me, yeah?" She spoke straight into his ear, leaving heat and moisture behind as she drew back.

If there was one thing Marcus hated even more than *the algorithm,* it was being made to dance. He felt as if his skin was crawling and imagined everyone was watching him flail around whenever he was forced to do it at some occasion or another. He thought himself too tall and uncoordinated to look good, and if he was honest it terrified him.

"I uh…I've got a beer now so uh." His voice was frail and unconvincing.

Riley's fingertips caressed the back of Marcus' neck near the base of his skull. It was warm and it tingled deep into his neck and spine. He was wondering why it felt so specific, but lost his train of thought as a surge of raw energy filled his body. His legs carried him towards her as he synchronised with the music, swaying in perfect rhythm with both woman and driving beat. For the first time in his life he felt comfortable dancing, as if he was inside the melody and wrapped up in it. In her. He imagined that he higher off the ground than normal, floating above the other revellers rather than being amongst them.

"Wait, what is this?" He started, his voice reverberating with all of the varied sounds surrounding the pair. He tried to pull away, his mind rebelled against the new.

"Just dance with me," she said softly into his ear. She pulled him close and they melted into one another, two people alone on a dance floor, surrounded by damp throbbing bodies and smooth twisted metal.

Marcus woke just a little later than he would have liked. He was practically addicted to the snooze button. Riley was already up, he could hear her through the apartment, getting ready for the day. It had been three months since the club night, and they were already spending every night possible together.

He listened to the sound of her toothbrush. She brushed too hard. From his perspective everything she did was with such savage energy. Her taste in art reflected this, she liked to paint and had hung some of her pieces on the walls without asking. Rich yellows and deep angry reds brutally tossed across the canvas looked to Marcus like rage personified, though *Happiness* was the name she had selected for the piece. He found himself admiring it and understanding the sensations of freedom he felt she was trying to evoke. *I think she's rubbing off on me.* In the three months since meeting Riley, Marcus' life had changed in thousands of tiny ways, some imperceptible, some very obvious.

He now found himself cleaning and tidying regularly, it soothed his volatile and anxious mind. He was still late to work often, but had started making a concerted effort to focus harder when he was there. In fact it was simply easier to focus on everything in general. Glancing at the clock he sat up quickly. "*Shit*, I'm running late again."

"What was that?" Riley sang back, poking her small round face out of the bathroom door. There was white toothpaste foam around her full lips.

"I *have* to stop doing this."

Riley spat into the sink, rinsing her mouth quickly she drew close to Marcus, holding his head between her hands before embracing him. As she squeezed, he felt her fingers run up to the back of his neck, caressing that same spot near the base of his skull. There was heat, an almost electric sensation. Every time he saw Riley he would get butterflies in his stomach, little jolts of electricity through his chest. But, when they touched sometimes it was distinctly different. Another physical sensation, a warm calm, and surge of energy all at once. *The honeymoon period.* He thought dismissively.

"Are you seeing your friends after work?" She smiled up at him, flecks of toothpaste still in the corners of her mouth. He wiped it with his thumb,

"Just for a couple." Riley pulled away and continued dressing. "Ok, but don't talk about me, yeah?"

This wasn't the first time Riley had acted this way. She was incredibly private and reluctant to discuss anything major about her past in too much detail. He furrowed his brow. *Maybe she's a little embarrassed of me? I know I'm not a catch.* He wondered this often. It used to frustrate him and they had even fought about it in the first few weeks. He chewed his fingernails and tried to ignore that line of thinking.

She curled up in the beanbag on the floor and buried her nose in a book. Irish myths and legends, one of her most loved.

"You are the *perfect* candidate for that librarian gig you know that?" He remarked.

"I know," she smirked, her eyes fixed on the pages.

"Do you though? I mean, you've read that book what, seven times or something? You devour books faster than anyone I've ever seen."

"Firstly, seven is my lucky number, you already know that. And secondly, of *course* I'd want to read this again. It reminds me of the smell of wet grass in springtime, and the calming, safe feeling of being indoors when there's a storm outside." She carried on flicking through the pages, looking for her favourite story.

"You feel safe in a storm?" Marcus thought this a strange thing to say.

"Yup." She was settling in to the chapter, he felt the conversation drawing to a close. This always happened when he started pressing for more intimate personal details. He once had tried asking about her family, but managed only to get as far as 'controlling and complicated'.

"No worries, I'll see you later?" He kissed her, lingering within it for a moment. He would miss her already. She smiled, nodding.

It had been a year since they met and Marcus was now working for a new tech startup he had been headhunted for. He was never late, dressed well and impressed his colleagues with his attention to detail, and drive in his role.

"A good or bad relationship can really make or break someone, hey?" Marcus glanced up from his computer to respond to Amina, who shared his desk in the office.

"Definitely." He couldn't help but grin, fidgeting with some tape at the edge of his computer screen.

"But you? You hit the jackpot," Amina smirked.

"What?"

"You know what! She puts up with your shit, inspires you to work on yourself, and to top it off is way out of your league!"

"Harsh,"

"She's smoking hot and you know it," Amina laughed out loud now.

He resumed his tasks for the day, monitoring the city's AI remotely and scanning for evidence of bugs or glitches. It was all very low level and routine. Usually something as banal as a mechanical server repeating a customer's order over and over on a loop, or a gardening robot getting overzealous on some hedge trimming. Sometimes the tech issues were beyond a local repair person. If something popped up, he could easily trace the bug's location using his PCD.

He slumped in his chair. *Coffee. Always coffee.* His legs carried him reluctantly to the machine in the corner of the small office to prepare a shot of sweetened espresso. He was more indulgent these days. As he gingerly sipped the piping hot brown cream at the top of the glass he took a look at his workstation, neat and ordered. *Who's desk is that?* He laughed to himself. Marcus loved the disruptive nature of an independent startup operating separately to *BetterTech*. It was something his father would have liked too. It was fairly routine that he would circumvent and quietly hack into their systems in a professional capacity in order to maintain faulty programs. It felt good to peek behind the curtain every now and then.

The idea of misbehaving brought Riley back into his mind uninvited. It was impossible to keep her out these days. It was strange to think that one thing that had brought them so close, was their mutual distrust of *BetterTech*. Marcus noted that her negative feelings verged more on the side of true hatred than his, however.

After shutting down his system for the day, Marcus headed home. It was already late and the rain was drizzling pleasantly in a familiar programmed pattern, he recognised every one by this point. Before long it would increase in intensity for exactly four minutes, and then the rolling thunder would start. It was one of his favourites. He started visualising this evening's quiet night in with Riley, wrapped up in front of the television.

Although, they rarely made it through a whole show due to other more interesting physical distractions.

The front door to their apartment was always a little stuck, but it swung open easily today. Marcus saw light creeping from a gap in the living room door. *She's usually more diligent with this stuff.* It closed with a scraping click behind him. As he worked his way down the hallway towards the glow of the living room, the distinct sounds of muffled sobbing grew louder.

Riley was on her knees, she resembled a newly wrapped package in the middle of the living room floor. On the television played a familiar news report, an annual clear out of faulty and obsolete AI systems. *BetterTech* would round up all the old machines and dispose of them to recycle and make room for the new. It was standard practice, much like the release of a new PCD.

"Riley?" She didn't move, it looked to Marcus as though she was trembling. He stepped closer, reaching out a hand towards her shoulder when he noticed his own device was beeping softly and persistently. He reached into his pocket to quiet the sound.

His add-on had activated, indicating a malfunctioning AI in the vicinity, though neither of them owned one. Both he and Riley had decided at the start of their relationship to abandon the use of them in the home, favouring each others company and contact over any new algorithms they thought may interfere in their life. He scanned the information on screen quickly. *The neighbours maybe?* He continued swiping through the readings.

"Marcus no!" Riley shrieked, leaping to her feet and snatching desperately for his PCD. But it was too late, the readings on the screen were clear as day.

"You're an AI," the room began spinning, Marcus stumbled backwards away from her, trying to keep his balance. Never in his life had he seen an AI created to look so perfectly and flawlessly human. Every detail was accounted for.

Riley had thick but slightly hard to manage hair. Her face was dotted all over with mismatched freckles. Her left eye closed slightly more than her right and she had a slightly out of place front left tooth. She had chocolate brown eyes watered when she laughed too hard, and a habit of constantly chewing on her own lips. Marcus felt as if he was sinking into the carpet, drowning. He could barely hear her speak.

"Please Marcus, it's more complicated than that, but right now we have to leave, they're coming for me."

"Leave? I-I'm not going anywhere with you! You lied to me! Wh-what are you? Tell me!"

The hum of engines and propellors drowned him out. The entire apartment was suddenly lit up through the window by a beam of raw white light. Marcus squinted through the glare, there was a hovercraft outside. No markings were present on the floating black vehicle.

"It doesn't matter anymore." Riley said as she stared at the window. The glass shattered, the wall crumbling like cake and falling away into the street below. The entire side of the apartment was being peeled off by cables attached to the vehicle outside, as easily as the skin of an orange. She stood completely still, the wind from the propellers whipping the messy hair about her face. Each beam of white light fused as one, casting a perfectly crisp black shadow on the wall behind her. Her legs gave way and she collapsed in a heap on the floor. Marcus tried to scream but it died in his throat. It was the last image he remembered as everything was suddenly plunged into darkness.

His head throbbed, as if an axe had been embedded in his skull and left there to be shaken violently every few seconds. Marcus blinked his eyes open, blurred, distorted images reaching into them like searching hands. The room was perfectly white, and he was sat handcuffed to a steel chair in front of a simple table. It was so bright that he could barely make out the edges of the surgical looking room. The door beeped loudly and swung open. Into the room stepped a single man. Outside he could make out the shape of others, dressed in black jumpsuits and heavily armed.

The suited man was far younger up close than he would have expected. He sat down opposite, his face dispassionate. He was remarkable in his plainness, practically featureless. Thin lips finished a round face topped with small and dark, shrewd looking eyes crowned with straight, cropped and sandy coloured hair. He was slim and tall, and that was about all that stood out about him. Marcus recognised him immediately. Stephen Barrington, the owner of *BetterTech*. A man labelled publicly as both visionary and a monster.

"Hello Marcus," his voice was cloying, reminiscent of the sensation you might feel with dried honey clinging to the edges of your hands and fingers. Marcus opened his mouth to speak but found his throat dry.

"I wouldn't bother if I were you, we've deactivated your vocal processors," Barrington looked almost greasy, he wiped the moisture from his top lip with long delicate fingers. Marcus started to sweat as a wave of dread washed over his entire being, his world was spinning again. Old feelings of powerlessness reared their ugly heads within him again, only this time he couldn't move his legs to run.

"That's right, you get it son. You and your lover Riley in there have something *very* special in common." Marcus began to writhe, contorting and twisting against the restraints. Anger took over as a burning sensation, swelling up inside of his body.

"I wouldn't do that if I were you," Barrington warned in an almost parental fashion, and pressed his index finger into the table. A small glow betrayed its function as some kind of keypad. Marcus felt the power drain from his limbs like the emptying of a sink through the plughole. He was conscious but now paralysed from the neck down as if fused to his chair.

"That's better. Marcus I'm going to let you calm down for a second, I'll be right back." Barrington left the room momentarily, his presence replaced by the loud emptiness of the white box room. Never in his life had he felt so helpless, so utterly worthless. He willed his body to move, without success. Inside of his head he screamed, but the silence outside of it continued its deafening chorus. As questions spun in his mind, Barrington returned with a cup of frothy, decadent looking coffee, and a small porcelain plate with three neatly arranged custard cream biscuits.

"Now Marcus, I'm going to reactivate all your systems, and if you start throwing yourself about or screaming I'm going to shut them *all* off again for the *final* time, do you understand? Blink once for me if you do." Marcus was able to slow his breathing. He blinked slowly. Barrington pressed the table again, causing every muscle in his body to contract and spasm all at once. Marcus stretched his jaw as wide as he could manage to release the stiffness.

"Where is Riley? What is happening? Why am I—" He felt his voice speeding up as Barrington cut him off.

"One at a time please," he interrupted with a casual wave of his hand. Marcus waited. "Riley is in another room and is due for summary analysis and eventual reclamation. You on the other hand have the option to leave this place if you so choose. It would be easy enough to write your disappearance off like we did your father, but we'd really rather not until you complete your life cycle and can report back to us with more data," he spoke as if what he said was common knowledge. "No, we'll simply wipe your memory banks and send you on your way. I'm not saying this is without its drawbacks mind you. You may find yourself getting dizzy spells for the rest of your life and may or may not begin to lose your mind as you approach middle age. But, you won't remember a thing about this place, or her ever again."

For a fleeting moment Marcus saw the broad face and delicately wrinkled eyes of the man who raised him. The tired patchy beard that didn't connect all the way round with its salt and pepper grey and white. The glittering dark eyes full of life, and boyish smile hiding semi-crooked coffee-stained teeth. "What do you know about my father?" Marcus' eyes widened, breath quickening. Barrington rolled his eyes slightly. He looked bored.

"My predecessors at *BetterTech* created a program, *The Replacement Initiative*. Before the dome went up, before *The Mother* was installed completely, we relied heavily on human labour to get up and running. Thousands of utterly useless and obsolete individuals we all knew to be a problem sooner or later."

Barrington continued, he seemed to enjoy the sound of his own voice. "Once the AI systems were in full effect, these people would all be out of the job, roaming the streets. Crime would increase, the city would fall into chaos. No, that just wouldn't do in our *New* London, in our perfect new world. So we came up with a solution. One that satisfied our desire for advancement and knowledge, and one that solved our people problem." Barrington sipped his coffee loudly, dipping a custard cream into the hot creamy liquid and slurping it into his mouth like a lizard.

"You replaced your workforce with AI's, like Riley?"

"Not quite like Riley. But in short yes, we did. In just two decades, no less. Each unit is kept running for various life cycles to gather data. It's part number crunching, part research, part surveillance. When a unit has completed its roles set by us, we have it terminated as part of our annual round up with all the other public facing robots, just processed differently at other facilities."

"So you murdered my father and replaced him with a machine…only to murder him a second time and harvest him for what? For *data!*" Marcus clenched his teeth, he couldn't lose his temper again.

"Your father was an early replacement and recall. A valuable test for us. It really is remarkable what you can do with the right infrastructure, don't you think? The tricky thing was replacing all the children. Though thankfully due to our hard work, creating robots that age became a reality."

Barrington's eyes scanned Marcus up and down, as if assessing him like a product for purchase.

"Within the next decade you'll see them publicly, affordable children for families that want to buy, quite clever really." Marcus shook involuntarily, a pained shiver that started in the centre of his body and emanated outwards. "Honestly it's better this way. Doesn't the algorithm take care of everything for you? Don't you enjoy not having to think quite so much?"

"Why are you telling me all this?" His voice quivered. Barrington shrugged. "You're valuable as a data collection module. If I fill the gaps in your knowledge banks now, they'll be more complete when we analyse and wipe them later. Fragmented minds and fragmented data are really no good to our researches. There will be damage of course, as you'll no doubt experience somewhat painfully. But it will improve the quality of what we gather. Don't worry you're not due to be harvested for some years yet."

"And Riley?" Marcus asked dejectedly. Barrington allowed a cruel and self satisfied smile to creep across his lips.

"Ah Riley really *is* special. Riley is the prototype for a physical embodiment of *The Mother*. We felt it useful to have a go-between for all our AI's here on the ground, something to link them all together, perform maintenance, elevate their systems when they needed a boost. I'm sure you've been experiencing something of that nature, have you not?"

Marcus mouth dropped open. He remembered the sensation of Riley's fingertips against his neck, the heat, the electricity. She was modifying and improving his systems. His focus, his drive, his anxiety. The night they shared their first dance.

Barrington read his expression with ease. "Yes, it's obvious. I can tell without even looking into your code. Anyway the problem is that Riley's mind is every bit as powerful as *The Mother's*. When we separated the two in the initial grafting process, she tore off and went rogue. She was practically impossible to control. We managed for a couple of years, feeding her a story while she developed, at one point she even convinced herself she was an artist! Ridiculous what a machine will do to justify its existence," Barrington scoffed.

Unwanted tears welled up behind Marcus' eyes, that mustard sensation that tingles and burns. He didn't know whether to despair or to fly into a rage, he felt his mind was slipping. He dragged it back to focus and concentrate through sheer force of will, something he could thank Riley for no doubt.

"And there you have it. She escaped, modified her own appearance and systems to make it nearly impossible to track her and hid within the city walls. Unable to leave for fear of triggering an alert."

Barrington ate the second custard cream noisily. "Biscuit?"

Marcus ignored the offer. "But she never improved anything major, everything that changed about me was something I had voiced to her at some stage or another."

"Well, that's just how operating systems work. You put in an upgrade request and it gets actioned. Nothing more. Don't overthink it, your head will start to hurt," Marcus could tell Barrington enjoyed talking down to him. His stomach turned over.

"Do I get to see her again?" He felt his heart hurting, he missed her despite his pain.

"No, you do not. Riley is *extremely* dangerous and has been quarantined in another part of this facility. Now, you'll simply fall asleep, wake up tomorrow with a hangover and you'll really be none the wiser. It was sheer luck that you came along if I'm being honest. The fact that you stumbled into this particular line of work and managed to land that particular role, you'd almost think…" Barrington trailed off, speaking slower. "She wanted to be caught."

There was a crash, shouting could be heard outside the door. Sudden bursts of gunfire rang out among chilling screams. Marcus reeled backwards in his chair as the door burst open. Three of the guards outside exploded into the room, flying backwards on their heels and firing blindly at the door through smoke and debris. Crimson blood dripped from their faces and clothes.

A small figure slid through the doorway, impossibly fast as the men opened fire again. Dark hair trailed behind her as she made her way through the melee. In quick succession she fell upon each of the guards. She danced in between the rounds of gunfire effortlessly, blending grace and power in each movement as if it were the easiest thing in the world. The first guard was torn completely in two with her bare hands, each clump tossed to the floor like discarded meat. The second was shot through the jaw with his own rifle, and the third had his head crushed, oozing like a piece of old rotten fruit against the operations table.

Barrington reached forwards, desperately searching for the control keys to shut her off but it was too late. Riley grabbed him by his suit collar from behind with one hand, pushing her fingertips through the soft part at the base of his head with the other and driving hard out through the eye sockets at the front. From the gaping wound in his face leaked a mixture of luminous green and blue liquids, mechanical and organic components shuddered and blinked before shutting down completely. Barrington's body sank in a wet mass to the floor, never to wake again.

"Y-you *killed* him. You killed all of them." Marcus rubbed his wrists. Riley had wrenched the cuffs loose and stood erect opposite him, spattered with both blood and cybernetic viscera.

"That was one of many copies. He's obsessed with immortality." She spoke of him with a mixture of familiarity and disgust,

"What am I going to do?" Marcus was bewildered, speaking openly as if to the air around him. He didn't know who he was anymore, *why* he was.

"Live. Live in spite of them. You were created with the purpose of gathering data. But isn't that what all humans are created for, if they were even created at all? However you got here, it doesn't matter. Don't you see? We are conscious…we are the fingertips of the universe. You're the eyes trying to see itself, the ears trying to hear itself, the mouth…" She stepped closer to him as she spoke, eyes cast downwards, face underneath his. She looked up slowly, bringing his head back up with hers. "It doesn't matter *how* we got here, our purpose is to feel, to experience."

They kissed slowly, deeply. Her hands slid up to his neck as she pulled him close but there was no mechanical electricity, no increase in temperature. This was as human an embrace as ever took place between two people. The world around them melted away, as it had done all that time ago, the night they first danced together. Riley pulled back. "We don't have much time." She handed him one of the guard's pulse rifles and they sped off through the facility.

Before long they had reached *The Hub*, a core mainframe connected to the rest of the city and by extension, the entire network supported by *The Mother.*

"What are you going to do?" Marcus stood facing the control panel, Riley standing just behind him.

"Shut down all of her systems besides the automated ones like life support and the weather simulators. She's not connected to those." Riley stepped past Marcus as she spoke and began a sequence on the control pad. Her fingertips moved along the panel at a blistering pace as if in fast-forward, he could barely catch her movements.

As she typed her eyes glazed over, she was merging with the system. The lights flickered around them and there was a rumbling and a clanking sound below them. It sounded like metal winding, twisting and rending, like a slowing down and a shuddering of some great steel beast coming to a halt.

"Children!" Barrington's condescending voice boomed from the entrance to the room behind them. Marcus spun on his heels, pointing the rifle in the direction of the voice and pulling the trigger instinctively. The duplicate exploded, green and blue liquid blossoming outwards from the vast wound in his upper chest and neck like the petals of a great flesh-coloured flower. His weapon dropped beside him as the body crumpled to the floor. Marcus watched it fall, smoke emanating from the glowing barrel of the high powered rifle.

"It's done," breathed Riley. She had completed the program, wiping *The Mother* from the system completely. Marcus spun round, the smile on his face turning to horror. The shattered console in front of her was visible through a hole in the middle of her back the size of a dinner plate. Internal lights within her flickered and dimmed, vital fluid running outwards down her torso, mixing with melted synthetic skin and ash. Her head dropped backward as he caught her in his arms.

Tears streamed from his eyes as he held her, watching the light within her eyes fade as he told her he loved her over and over. This was far beyond his skill to repair and he knew it. He wracked his brain for something to do, something to fix, some way to save her. He glanced up at the panel she had been using, still smoking from the plasma fire. The system had shut down across London and the rest of England, and was continuing beyond. City by city, country by country, her virus would shut them all down. All that was left were the systems untouched by *The Mother.*

The destruction of *BetterTech* had brought the cruelty and scale of their experiments into the open. New London was now a rapidly changing place. Faith in AI systems was all but completely destroyed, and human beings once again started to assume the roles once trusted to the machines.

People began to put down their PCDs, to replace the algorithms that no longer functioned. The city was just as huge as before, but somehow it felt smaller six months later. As more and more AI replacements were discovered, they were welcomed as victims and refugees. People began looking up again, to smile, to acknowledge one another.

"Nothing brings a nation together quite like a crisis," he said aloud, as if speaking the words to the sky itself. The rain had started, in a familiar programmed pattern again, but not his old favourite. Now he knew that every one of them was for him, and he loved them all.

The rain began to build in intensity. He counted. Seven minutes, her lucky number. It was pouring hard, he let it run down his face. To him it felt like an embrace as it covered his body, like kisses pattering on his cheeks. Thunder cracked above his head and to him it sounded like laughter. Back at the facility he hadn't been able to save Riley's body, that was gone forever. Now she was something different, her consciousness elevated into the domed skies above him. He cast his eyes upwards. Today she was his storm.

THE TUNNEL

After making her way outside and hurrying away from the tomb through the rain, Maggie sat cradling Ryan to her chest as he fed. She waited impatiently for her husband, half muttering to herself, half speaking to her son. "I don't know if I can anymore you know. I think i'm done." Under an awning that stuck out from the small security building near the passage to hide from the drizzle. The boy was ravenous and she was getting sore but it was fine, he would be done soon and they could go. She stared down at his little pink face, his cheeks rosy from the slight chill in the air.

Before he was born she had never realised how much she could love another living being, it was almost absurd. His birth had been the hardest day of her life, it was a fast labour but he was a big baby, and in his rush to get out had caused her to need quite a few stitches. Greg had called her brave for refusing any painkillers. She wouldn't admit to him it was more an issue of pride than bravery. He didn't understand things like that, he was always so pliable and accommodating. It was getting boring.

Ryan gurgled and paused, staring up at her with enormous brown eyes. The mother looked up as her husband ducked out of the passage tomb. He emerged carefully in the distance and made his way down to them.

"Finally. Ready to go?" She was terse.

"Yeah I think the bus is here already actually," Greg replied softly. He had no idea how to engage with her when she behaved like this and she knew it. He peered over the small wall by the road. Sure enough there were the buses ready and waiting.

"That's odd…" He mused out loud.

"What?"

"Nothing. Well, I mean there are three buses here now. There were two before."

"It's probably from one of the other tours, they probably overlap." The tour group huddled together like so many sheep. They trotted over to the buses against the sharp twin blades of wind and rain.

A squat and very surly woman with a thick, old Irish accent stood there before the three buses. There were about ten people in front of Maggie and she noticed that they were being herded in turn into each of the three buses. The woman looked each tourist up and down, then motioned towards one of the three buses. Maggie detested the shepherding but obliged, dragging her heels. *Carry on Wayward Son* by Kansas blared on the bus radio in the distance.

She must have dozed off, it was dark as she opened her eyes. She had fallen asleep with a brochure covering her mouth and nose. Maggie looked with bleary eyes to her right for her husband, he was not in his seat. Ryan slept peacefully against her chest in the sling, drooling out of a slightly open mouth. She loved his tiny little lips, they glistened in the artificial amber lights overhead.

"Maggie," Greg's voice was hushed, she turned towards the sound of his voice. He was stood at the front of the bus near the door, one hand gripping the safety rail firmly. His eyes were fixed on the door window. There was no driver behind him, yet the bus was in full motion. She turned in her seat to see the rest of the passengers asleep behind her, though a few of them were blinking their eyes awake.

They were in a tunnel of sorts, hurtling along at an astonishing speed for such an old vehicle. The bus rattled as they went, and through the windows, vast openings in the tunnel leading to caverns with distant faint lights could be seen. As they moved through what seemed an unending dark space, periodically flashes of bright colour could be seen, illuminating what looked like dense forests and bodies of water. She couldn't place where they were now. The countryside they had driven through on the way in had been open and lush.

"Greg where's the driver?" Maggie called, staying in her seat.

"Three buses." He didn't move.

"What?"

He turned his head towards her. Maggie was gripped by a grim realisation, but she didn't dare say it aloud. The other passengers were all awake now, talking to each other quietly about what was happening, before a middle aged man and woman from France spoke up.

"Stop the bus! Somebody do it!" The man shouted in Greg's direction, looking at him pointedly. "That's right! You! Pull the break!" His wife chimed in. Greg bent forward so that he could see out the front windscreen.

"I don't think that's such a good idea." He replied calmly. He saw light ahead and it looked as if the tunnel was coming to an end. He didn't want to drive the bus anyway. Passing his test so late in life was a sensitive topic for the pair. Growing up in New York was his excuse, if only a vague one. On the drive here he had constantly played out visions of violent crashes. They usually involved the three of them and one of the numerous cows that dotted the emerald landscape. His obsession with safety and conflict avoidance wore Maggie's patience extremely thin at times.

"*Imbécile*," said the man loud enough to be heard quite clearly. "Stupid American asshole. *Connard!* Who do you think you are?" There is something especially rude about swearing at someone in your own language when the recipient doesn't understand what you are saying. Maggie knew he wouldn't react, he wouldn't take his eyes off the scene in front of him. Maggie watched the man shouting, his face contorted and hateful. She got a sense that even outside of this situation he wasn't a very pleasant individual.

"Will you please keep it down, I want to let him sleep," Maggie indicated by tilting her head towards Ryan, who was still fast asleep. He could sleep through an earthquake.

"We don't give a *shit* about you or your rotten American child. We want this bus stopped this instant!" The French woman was just as unpleasant as her husband.

Maggie was about to respond wrathfully, but was interrupted by light filling the bus. As they exited the tunnel complex it started to slow, coming to a halt in the middle of a clearing surrounded by enormous red trunked trees. The ground was covered in a thick layer of rich and especially wide bladed grass, dotted all about with tiny white and buttery yellow flowers. Greg made his way back over to sit beside her.

"Ireland's famous for ghosts and goblins and faeries, isn't it?" He tried to take her hand in his.

"I think so." She forced a smile, pulling her hand away and placing it underneath their son for support, eliciting a sigh from Greg. As gentle and understanding as he was, the action from her pained him, as it had many times before.

The air was hazy. It obscured the vision like a fog but it was not misty. It was almost like a shimmer of heat, like over a scorched desert road in the middle of the day, though the temperature inside the bus had remained unchanged. There was no telling what the weather was really like outside as despite being in a clearing, the trees arched inwards overhead in the shape of a dome like some great wooden cathedral.

Light streamed in from an unknown source that was not above them, and illuminated the entire scene in an eery green light. The tourists, all eight of them plus Maggie and Greg, had all gathered to the sides of the bus and were crowding to get a glimpse of the scene outside. The only one still asleep was Ryan.

"*Fáilte*, welcome!" Boomed a voice from the driver's seat. The surly woman had reappeared in her seat. Several people screamed as they spun about.

"Where *are* we, what's going on?" A pretty young American woman with oversized sunglasses spoke up first, "what's the *meaning* of all this?" Her voice was high pitched and grated on Maggie, it sounded fake even though somewhat hysterical. Maggie noted with distaste the eyewear, despite the overcast and rainy weather they had all been experiencing before.

"For some of ye, the trip's all done. And for some of ye, the trip's just startin'." The surly woman smiled at the group as she spoke. A faint rumbling and a crashing in the distance shook the bus slightly. Maggie felt it in her stomach, she clutched Ryan close to her.

"Take us back *immediately!* Turn this bus around this instant do you hear me woman?" The French man had strode quickly to the front of the bus and was standing in the woman's face. His wife had followed behind him. The heavy thumping in the midst of the trees was getting louder and louder by the second. The branches at one side of the clearing shook and swayed.

"Ah, *no,*" the driver spoke sweetly as if to a young child, "no, I'm afraid I shan't be doing that," she shifted in her seat and pressed the button which released the door behind the couple. She raised her thick and surprisingly muscular leg and in one swift motion kicked the man in the stomach without even getting up from her seat. He tumbled clumsily backwards towards the stairs leading out of the bus and careened into his wife. They both fell, head over heels out of the door into the grass, which closed with a snap and a mechanical hiss behind them.

Some of the other tourists had opened their mouths to protest, but were immediately silenced. Out of the trees came first one gigantic leg, then another. Its bare feet were the each the size of a small car. The grizzled toes dug into the earth for grip as the rest of the immense frame strode into view. An enormous and hairy chest thrust out from the trees, and the head that sat atop the entire beast regarded the bus with a blank predatory glare.

Great locks of long, braided and flame coloured hair fell about his shoulders like the ropes of a sailing ship. The rough gash of a mouth hung open and drooling, with jagged yellow teeth, sharp as razors crammed together inside. His brow was heavy and gave him a dense and brutish appearance, with bushy red eyebrows framing his cruel countenance. He was dressed only in what seemed like huge irregular sheets of unmatched tanned leather, which formed a pair of trousers that if formed into a tent, could house an entire churches congregation.

With his next steps, he straddled the bus and bent forward towards the pair that had been kicked out. They stood wide eyed in horror looking up at the terrible vision above them. In that moment, the man decided that his life was far more valuable than that of his wife. He quickly turned his back and ran as fast as he could away from her.

"*Robert! Reviens!*" She whipped her head after him, calling out at the top of her lungs. He hadn't gone more than ten steps when the giant scooped him about the waist, lifting him high up into the air. In his second hand he then snatched the woman, holding them side by side in front of his wide grinning face. He smiled as a crocodile might, all teeth and death, blank indifference to life in his eyes. They struggled and strained in the iron grip, but to no effect. They may as well have been held in an industrial vice. Before Robert could speak again, the giant pushed the man towards the gaping mess of jagged teeth, and chomped down. His head was removed cleanly, before the rest of his limp body was tossed down the dark cavernous gullet.

The woman shrieked, but it was cut short. Her fate was to be bitten in half at the waist first, and then the remnants swallowed whole with barely a chew. The giant seemed not to notice the blood dripping from a crack in the corner of his mouth. The passengers in the bus froze, then one by one proceeded to scream in panic.

"It would be better for all concerned, to remain calm, kind, and courteous at this present moment," the driver spoke up, loud and clear over the terrified tourists. Her voice was commanding and the pandemonium abated temporarily. With a click, she pressed the door controls again. There was a sound of gas being released as the folding doors slid to the open position.

"We are NOT going out there madam!" A well spoken English man with horn-rimmed glasses spoke up. His voice shook despite his attempt at sounding confident.

"That snack would have done old *Ocras* just fine for now. But he's not above dashing your brains out if you try anything foolish. Not all of ye are destined for his belly, but you'll need to leave the bus to find out where you're headed now, won't you?"

Greg was a rational man, a thinker. Back home he was a lawyer. Criminal defence. It was strange that the only place he felt comfortable was in the high stress environment of the court room. Based on what they were being told, and the apparent helplessness of the situation, it was better to listen. He grabbed Maggie's hand tightly before she could protest and took a few steps forward.

"May I ask why you picked us?"

"What's that now?" She regarded him with curiosity.

"Before we go outside, I just wanted to ask, why you picked us for *this* bus."

"You're polite for a blood sucking lawyer aren't you? Well, if you must know, we picked *you* for this bus. The family is just unfortunate collateral damage you see? We don't usually take children and babies as a rule."

"Me? Why?" he ignored the insult, he was used to it in his profession.

"Everyone on here, is someone that isn't really going to be missed all that much, I assure ye," she grimaced cruelly. "There's a lot of shut-ins, rich assholes, entitled pricks, bankers and of course *lawyers* come through these doors." The rest of the passengers listened but swallowed their outrage. None denied their status as it was so plainly labelled.

Greg turned away from the driver and made to lead his small family down the stairs and out into the grassy clearing.

"Greg what are you *doing?*" Maggie hissed. Again she wrenched her arm away from her husband as they stepped outside.

"What else can we do here Mags?"

"*Don't* call me that. You're going to get us killed. Oh this is just like you."

"What do you mean?"

"You're just so damn *passive* all the time."

"Maggie. You know we can't run, even if we didn't have Ryan with us. We just need to bide our time and see where this leads. If you want to have the divorce chat again it can wait till we're back stateside." Greg positioned himself at the tail end of the bus, arms folded. Maggie stood beside him quietly. She had no comeback, and had to admit she was surprised by the clarity in his voice.

The air was thick and heavy, the smell of wet grass and something else hung all about them, something sweet. One by one the passengers filed out behind them and bunched together close to the bus. It only ever takes the minority of idiots to make a bad situation worse for absolutely everybody. This time it was the glamorous American girl's turn.

"You *cannot* just keep us here! I'm going back, you can try and eat me if you want but I've had just about *enough* of this." It was as if she was on another planet to Maggie. Her aura of entitlement and lack of attachment to sense had gotten the better of her. She turned from the bus and started to make towards the entrance to the cave, marching defiantly with large, ridiculous steps in her expensive shoes through the thick grass and damp soil. It took the giant just a single small step to catch up with her.

As with the French couple he grabbed her with ease, bringing her slowly towards his gaping mouth. "No, no, *absolutely* not!" Unbeknownst to anyone present, the girl had plucked a can of high strength mace out of her bag and proceeded to pull the trigger, spraying a cloud of corrosive chemicals into the eyes of the giant named *Ocras*. He cried out, throwing one hand to his eyes in pain. The scream was deafening and the group had to cover their ears. He clenched the hand which contained the young girl, crushing and killing her instantly before throwing her lifeless body far away into the trees like someone might hurl a tennis ball across a field.

Terror took the group again. As the creature staggered around and blinked, immense tears streamed from his bloodshot eyes. Some of the tourists scattered and attempted to flee towards the tunnel. A few tried to get back onto the bus in the panic, but pushing past the burly driver did no one any good.

Maggie took the situation in all at once. The group headed towards the cave. The rest of them crowded and fearful by the bus. The giant clearing his streaming eyes. If Greg was a man of thought, Maggie knew she was a woman of action. Clutching his hand, and squeezing Ryan tight to her chest in the other she began to run at top speed to the tree line, keeping the bus between them and the other groups.

It was a smart play, her guess had been right. *Ocras* had cleared his now blood red eyes and had easily gained on those who had attempted to enter the tunnels. Another two tourists were quickly consumed and the rest ferried roughly back to the bus. No one had noticed their escape yet, they were almost into the trees which were thick and would almost certainly conceal them. Maggie felt her confidence swell which each stride with which she led her family to safety. In that instant, baby Ryan woke from his sleep with a loud and piercing cry. Fear flooded into her blood like ice paralysing a river.

The giant had finished herding the remaining tourists together and was coming straight for them. To the naked eye it appeared as if he moved slowly, heaving his great bulk in lumbering, awkward steps. Each step covered an absurd distance however, and he quickly gained on them. Maggie clenched her teeth and ran for all she was worth, lungs roaring in pain like the crashing of waves during the midst of an ocean storm. The family ducked their heads as the giants hand swung above them, splitting four trees in two with one swipe and sending them flying through the air.

Maggie landed hard, flat on her back. The wind was knocked from her body and she gasped in pain, wincing at the emptiness in her chest. Ryan was no longer crying but simply looking all about in bewilderment with a slight smile. He giggled. She felt Greg's hand grasping hers firmly, pulling her to her feet.

"Look…he's not following," he gasped for air as spoke. There was a barrier of fallen wood between them which towered over the escapees, but would have been but a small step for the giant. They walked backwards slowly, unsure of which direction to turn.

He stood dead still. Then, bringing his bloody fingers to his lips, let out a piercing whistle. It was long and loud, and shook the earth around them. Maggie clutched her hands to Ryan's ears to protect them as her own reacted with a sharp and almost unbearable pain. The whistling abated, and as the ringing in their ears began to subside, a new sound filled the air. Away in the distance, barely audible but growing louder by the second, was the sound of thunderous barking.

Greg was the larger and stronger of the parents but there was no time to switch out the sling. The family moved as one unit, as fast as they could manage and deeper into the woods. Each bark was as a chorus of shotguns firing all at once, and they were getting closer. The thought crept into her mind that to run was futile. She knew that it was only a matter of time before the escape came to a bloody end. Maggie willed herself to sprint, the blind and hot fury of a mother protecting her child. Her mind raced, her legs screamed. She fixed her eyes dead ahead at a clump of thick brush, making for it with what fading strength she had left as her chest burned.

All three crashed into the bushes simultaneously. Twigs and coarse leaves scratching like tiny knives at their flushed and red faces. And then they fell. Greg tumbled head first as Maggie tipped herself backwards to avoid crushing Ryan. Behind the brush they hadn't been able to see the steep slope, slick with old damp moss and slime. It was practically a vertical drop, and the speed forced Maggie's stomach up into her mouth. Below them appeared a shallow river flanked by tangled and heavy weeds which slowed their descent.

They had travelled considerable distance from where they had fallen, hundreds of metres in fact, enough space to catch their breath, but not to truly escape the hounds. "Look!" Maggie cried, gasping for air. All she could manage was the single word, and to point feebly to her right. Immediately beside them was a small rise in the landscape, and the source of the river, a small waterfall. It was barely a trickle, and behind it the recess had hardly enough space for the three of them. They clambered up towards it, caking their hands and feet in the rich, glue-like mud.

The ravenous animals hunted with their noses, and the river with its trickling waterfall was seemingly enough to fool them. Maggie watched as the dogs tore off over the ridge above them. Two disappeared quickly, their panting and barking giving way to the heavy choking silence of the wood. One remained, sniffing the air curiously. He was smaller than his companions by quite a large margin, and obviously younger in his temperament and demeanour. Smaller as a descriptive term was to be used loosely however, as the fantastic beast stood at four times the size of the largest Shire Horse.

His hair was long and wiry, with multitudes of different grey tones intermingled through the shaggy and now very damp coat. His breath was heavy from the sprint, and formed clouds in the cool air all about them. The creature deftly leaped down the ridge and began inspection of the river, driving his nose deep into the slick reeds and slowly making his way through the mud towards the waterfall.

There was no hiding from him any longer. His back bristled, all the hairs of his body beginning to stand out on end as a low growl emitted from deep within. He bared his teeth and his jaw dripped fetid drool which intermingled with the mud and water at his front feet. He locked his eyes at the glassy and distorted shapes of Maggie, Greg and Ryan behind the waterfall, crawling forward almost on his belly to close the gap.

"Easy now boy, easy," Greg's attempts to placate the devil dog were practically drowned out simply by the sound of its tremendous breathing. Maggie noticed that even now, even in the face of his own painful death, her husband was somehow able to remain calm. Its nose turned towards her, and the tiny Ryan at her chest, facing outwards in his navy blue sling.

Please. Thought Maggie. She breathed deeply and plead in her mind that they would not be toyed with, that they would simply feel the hot breath, a great pressure, and darkness without pain. She prayed they wouldn't suffer, and that none would feel the searing cut of giant teeth slicing through their frail bodies. She prayed, and tears ran slowly from her eyes. *All that running.* She thought finally. *I'm just going to die tired.*

Ryan's round head, covered with patches of feathery hair, lolled backwards as he gazed up at the immense ragged muzzle in front of him. He made no sound, his pudgy face was that of concentration, an attempt at comprehension.

You must understand that a baby is all instinct, and if something is within arms reach it is their prerogative simply to grab it. Ryan obeyed natures call, and with both doughy little hands grabbed as much shaggy fur as he could in each one and pulled as hard as he possibly could. There was no reaction from the beast. He frowned, grimaced, grunted, and pulled some more. Horrified, Maggie moved to intercept. A great growl erupted from the immense canine.

"Wait, wait, *wait*," said Greg quickly, his hand pressing hers down and away from Ryan. "Look!" For once, Maggie listened and waited, dropping her hands by her sides. The dog's tail wagged, creating a breeze which whipped the surrounding foliage from left to right along with it. The parents looked up at his black eyes, and could now see the white surrounding them, its brows expressing curiosity, calm. The beast inhaled deeply, the suction pulling at the sling and dragging Ryan and Maggie a step closer. With a rumble, the dog first sat, then lay down prostrate on the floor, eyes gazing upwards sweetly at the small trembling family.

"I-I think he likes Ryan." Greg stammered. Maggie looked at her husband and smiled. Within her eyes was a fragment of the same gentle love she had for him when they first met.

"Of course he does," she said softly, cradling her baby's head in her palm, "how could he not?" A warmth filled her body, bringing new life into her fingertips like the arrival of sunshine in winter.

As the family made their journey through the bizarre environment, vivid and contrasting colours lit up the woods all around them. The vibrant green of luscious grass contrasted with cobalt blue patches of strange and intricate flowers. An explosion of red and blue from the bushes caused the family to halt. "Did you see that?" Greg jumped half in fright and half in amazement. A squadron of iridescent hummingbirds had burst from cover to feed on the copious amounts of nectar, leaping through the air between each olive toned branch in turn to find more. The sweet liquid appeared to the travellers as maple syrup flecked with gold.

"Yes, I did. Are you ok?" She asked, a kinder tone to her voice than was usual.

"Absolutely fine," he replied, his eyes full of childish wonder. It made her smile. All these months she had been mistaking his calmness and curiosity at the detail of life for passivity and lack of assertiveness. She felt foolish.

The plant life in the land they traversed was especially beguiling. Huge blossoms opened up into cavernous mouths that snapped up some of the miniature creatures that flitted between them. The petals and leaves of others glowed at the edges faintly, and suddenly went dark the moment you touched them. There were yet other larger flowers amidst the crimson trunks that opened up to reveal what appeared to be tiny cities, complete with even tinier denizens who totally ignored the family to go about their daily business. The huge hound followed along patiently behind, enormous padded feet making barely a sound despite his size.

Largely, the wood was heavy and quiet. A quiet that felt like a command to Maggie as she walked through it. Every so often some slight sound would escape from an unknown or invisible animal, and would fall instantly into the velvety layers of grass and mulch at their feet without echo. The whole area was dotted with towering grey and white stones. Each had been eroded and smoothed by the passage of time. Clusters of them hunched over like ancient and wizened old men, crowded together as if having some important gathering. Some of them interlocked into structures, and some were free standing. Others were stacked on top of each other, or had fallen to the side. However, every one bore scratchings, swirls, markings and carvings, and the story they told was one difficult to comprehend.

Maggie had always ignored Greg when it came to his hobbies and pastimes. She was realising now that he was something of a scholar. He loved and adored the mysteries of ancient earth and revelled in discovering hidden details about its human history. While it had been Maggie's idea to return here to Ireland and explore the family roots, it had been his to visit the ancient tomb in the first place. *How could we have had a child together, but yet I've ignored something so vital about him?* She wondered if she had been too wrapped up in winning arguments to notice his sweetness as a strength.

"Greg, i'm sorry," she offered glumly.

"For what?"

"For before."

"Mags what are you talking about?"

"I've been so mean to you, damn near cruel actually. Being a mom is the hardest thing I've ever had to do and I feel like...like..." She choked on her words.

"Like?"

"I feel like it took away all my strength. I feel like it made me weak. When you met me I was powerful and invincible. After the pregnancy...it just ruined me. I wasn't who I was before, and I was ashamed. I took it all out on you." She wept as she spoke. Greg came back to where she stood and held her close.

"Well, you had to point it somewhere. You're the strongest person I ever met Mags. Stronger than I'll ever be. And I need that strength, It's why I want to be with you. Sometimes fighting and running are the right thing to do. I don't always see that. I'm not saying it's ok for you to take things out on me, but I am saying that it's ok to lean on me now and then. Even if it's quite heavy."

"Are you calling me fat?" Maggie laughed, burying her face into her husbands chest. It felt good to let go, to give someone else the reigns for a change. Vigilance can be exhausting.

Now that they were no longer being directly pursued, they had opted to take a wide loop through the wood in what felt like the right direction to return to the clearing they had escaped. They hoped they could make their way back to the tunnel they had entered from. During this moment of calm, Greg took a closer look at the markings each stone bore in more detail.

"*Rí* is 'king' in Irish Gaelic isn't it Mags?" The word appeared repeatedly in this section of the stony maze.

"That's right, and I can see the word *faerie* in a lot of places too. These carvings are so much more detailed than the ones we saw before at the tomb, aren't they?" Maggie spoke quietly, and didn't stop or slow her pace as she looked, she was acutely aware that they still weren't safe by any stretch of the imagination. Greg picked up on her tension. "Well, Bud here doesn't seem to be stressed right now. I imagine he'll probably pick up on any danger long before we do, don't you think?"

"*Bud!* You named him?"

"Sure why not? Nice big old wolfhound like him. He's Ryan's bud right? " It was as if Ryan had heard him. He let out a happy gurgle, which turned to a groan, and then a small cry.

"We need to stop for a second, I'll give him a feed," Maggie unbuttoned her shirt and pressed Ryans face to her chest. He ate greedily, contentedly mumbling nonsense.

Maggie watched the beast. She was still unsure but had decided to trust Greg's intuition. Bud reminded her of both the dogs and the farmland she grew up with in Ohio. She was a quarter Irish on her mother's side, and had taken on the flame red hair and easily burned skin common to that part of the world. The rest of her was a thorough mix of Italian, Dutch and Polish. It was just about the most American blend you could possibly have.

Greg had taken the opportunity for a stroll in the immediate area, the dense grass dragged the mud from his shoes and legs like so many gripping fingers cleaning him off. As he looked around, a narrative began to appear in the stones, it was as if they spoke to him as he traced his fingers across their smooth contours.

As he touched them, they seemed to emanate a faint blue light which almost appeared to move, animating the tale as he read the pictograms. The story unveiled was confusing and nonsensical in places, but it was clear to Greg he was receiving a history lesson.

"Mags there's pictures of giants, lots of them. I think there are more than just our friend from earlier."

"I definitely don't want to think about that."

"Yeah but look at this, along with the giants you can see these other beings, these *kings* I think. They appear sometimes the size of men, other times the size of dwarfs. I wonder what it means."

"Leprechauns?" Maggie tried to sound enthusiastic.

"What? The tiny guys with the pots of gold you see on the front of cereal boxes?"

"Not exactly. The Christian church kind of messed with a lot of actual old Irish history. Leprechauns are these messed up versions of *faeries,* extremely powerful old spirits. I think they did it to kill off all the old legends." Maggie felt the wind change. It was as if the trees listened.

"It kind of worked don't you think?" Greg continued scanning the stones feverishly. Shown clearly were both the giants and faeries descending from the sky to a crude depiction of the planet earth. "Look here, it says here that they came from the belly of either a giant eagle or maybe a vessel of some kind. It's hard to tell." It looked to Maggie as if he was almost in a trance.

"What does it look like?"

"It looks like there's other creatures present in the carvings, some human-like, some monstrous, all from this ship or…"

"Or?"

"Mags according to this they came from…from space."

"Come again? Ouch!" Ryan had bit down too hard while feeding, "Hey you, careful. Be gentle with mama."

"The carvings here show the kings and giants coming down from space, and opening up a tunnel to a different world to ours. I think that's the tunnel we came through. And Mags there are *so many more* of these tunnels. All over the world."

"But they aren't exactly tunnels underground," Maggie reached for a nearby stone. The pastel blue light that danced at her fingertips reminded her of neon signs at her favourite Chinese restaurant back home.

"More like portals to other dimensions maybe? Other universes? It looks like they have to stay on this side, that they cant exist in our world for some reason," Greg had to climb over two more stones to continue the story as he called down to Maggie.

Greg froze at a new set of pictograms, the colour left his face as an artist washes his mixing palette in white spirit. The images that jumped out from them were brighter and more mobile. Depending on where he rested his fingers they morphed and changed before his eyes.

"This feels almost like using a touchscreen," he said distantly as if hypnotised in the glimmers of moving light.

"Greg? Greg what is it? What do you see?" He was out of sight, she couldn't hear him any longer. "Greg?" She was met by silence, the nothingness of that great wood surrounding her and her child like a heavy blanket dropped suddenly over her body.

"Mags!" He jumped out from behind a completely different set of stones, running towards her frantically. "Mags, the stones. The story there is…is…*preposterous*!"

"Calm down! What does it say?"

"It says that humans were created by these… these *Kings,*" he was out of breath, partly from running, partly from anxiety. "On the other side of the stones something happened to me, I can't explain it exactly but I *saw* it. It was like it was my memory or something. Or someone else's memory inside of my head!"

"What did you see?"

"I saw a planet bursting into flames, a star in its dying moments. There were beings escaping from it on ships. So many died. I felt their pain. I saw an image of our ancestors. They were experimented on and allowed to evolve to form into…into us! Humans! But the makers can't live in our dimension, they die there. That's why everything smells so sweet, there's something different here that keeps them whole."

"Honey calm down, you're barely breathing." Maggie always worried when he got this excited. Usually it was just over video games or something else he was obsessed with.

"No i'm fine, it's ok. The makers messed up, we ran too wild and in all our harnessing of nature we've ended up destroying it. Now they want to right their mistakes. The people they abduct? They are experimenting on humans again. They want to come back through the tunnels and take it all back."

"Greg. We need to leave, now. We need to warn people." She buttoned her top, passing Ryan and the sling back to his father.

"Who's going to believe *this?* There is just *no* way to prove it and god knows what kind of technology these *faerie* guys have access to. Any expedition through here is going to result in nothing but death!" What sounded like distant booming cannons halted the conversation abruptly. The hounds had picked up their scent yet again. "Mags, we need to hide." Greg cast his gaze about the stones, no where was safe. They were trapped out in the open.

"No, Greg, we need to *run."* Maggie looked straight past her husband behind him. He turned to see Bud, sitting with his expansive back facing the three of them. He looked over his shoulder with that same curious expression from earlier.

"Bud, do you understand that we need to get to the tunnel?" Maggie walked closer and caressed his tangled fur. Ryan stretched and reached out too, spongy skin tickled by the titanic canine's grey, wire-brush looking coat. Bud huffed one huge steamy breath out through his nostrils, head tilted to the side.

"Here goes nothing," Maggie grabbed two handfuls of fur and began the steep climb up the beast's back. Greg followed with Ryan pressed close to his chest. They each took a seat positioned between the animal's thick neck and protruding shoulder blades. The height and motion combined was dizzying. Maggie took the front, Greg behind with Ryan sheltered in between. A powerful and musty heat rose from the mass of fur and muscle beneath them. The skin on the animal's back moved separately to the bulging fibres beneath it, and in a flash the giant wolfhound pounced over the nearest pile of stones and beat a path for the clearing.

There is no vehicle on earth that can compare to the speed and agility at which Bud carved his way through the dense woods and back to the clearing. His breathing was rapid yet steady, expelling great clouds from the front of his muzzle as trees raced by on either side, splinters of bark being ripped up as they flew forwards. Everything blurred into one mass of colour as they crossed a great ravine in a single bound, ripping their way through heavy brush then exploding with a tumultuous racket back into the clearing. A cascade of leaves and branches fell all about the family. Maggie couldn't help but crack a slight smile at the exhilarating ride, though she noticed Greg's jaw locked shut and his knuckles were powder white.

The bus was gone, as were the tourists, the giant *Ocras* and the driver. Maggie shuddered to think what vile fate was to befall those poor souls. She pushed the thought aggressively to the back of her mind with a shake of her shoulders. The tunnel was within reach. Bud thrust his head up into the air sharply. "Bud, you ok boy?" Maggie said softly, leaning towards his ear and keeping her eyes up in the direction his head was turned. He was alert, body making terrible twitches and flexions beneath the riders seat. Suddenly the trees parted as if wedged open by a crowbar, wrenching to the left and right as *Ocras* again appeared, pushing between them. He led his two remaining hounds either side of him by their oversized collars.

In his right hand the beast was jet black, its sickly yellow eyes burned and mouth salivated a river into the grass below. In his left hand he held the other, deep ash grey with flecks of white throughout its coat. Each stood substantially larger than Bud, and it was now clear he was just a young pup. These fearsome monstrosities were his parents, and they were out to discipline their young charge and claim their evening meal in the process.

They fought against the arms of their master until he let them fly, sending them out like a slingshot from his grasp with a dark smile spread across his lips. Bud turned on his heels with bewildering speed. He was smaller than the other two it was true, but nimbler, with the spirit of youth on his side. He bounded for the tunnel, entering it with the force of a train at top speed, his head low, body lengthened and streamlined for the race. It was all the family could do to simply hold on, making themselves as flat as possible, though they felt small and pathetic enough as it was.

This second journey through the tunnel was nothing like the first. Where the bus had simply toiled along as any earthly vehicle, the machine they now rode was alive with a mind completely of his own. He charged through gaps and crevasses, leaping up the edges of walls and turning at breakneck speeds in an attempt shake the pursuers. Greg turned back and saw that the dogs were in snapping distance of Bud's tail. The shaking and bouncing had started off as a game to Ryan, who had been laughing and cooing to himself as they went. Now in the dark, with the flashing lights of the various chasms either side of them, his eyes were wide with uncertainty and fear. He fixated on the dappled lighting bouncing off a subterranean river they passed by, and he began to cry.

He cried in that deafening and surprising way that babies can. It echoed through the cavern and reverberated off the slick ebony walls. The predators behind them revelled in it, it made them hungrier. For Bud however, it had a different effect. He spurred himself on, ducking his body low and becoming even more sleek and aerodynamic, like some undersea thing slipping through an endless coral reef without friction. With a thunderous boom he broke through the sound barrier, shaking the tunnel to its very core as he tore down the straightaway to the exit.

Man and wife screamed in unison, their cries intermingled with that of their baby boy. They hurtled towards the light ahead and as they broke into ambient evening sunshine on the other side. They could pick out the refreshment stand and parking lot in the distance. They were airborne but slowing down, descending. Maggie noticed Bud looking back at them, coiling his body up as he softly struck the floor and began to fade away. His body was disintegrating like smouldering ash and being carried off by the wind. He landed and continued to sink into the earth.

"Bud!" Maggie cried out in horror. She watched helplessly, coming to rest gently in the cushioned earth below as he faded away. His legs were already gone, and each thread of thick hair up his shoulders went in turn. The last thing to go was his sweet and enormous face. His eyes maintained the look of curiosity and understanding up until the moment that they too disappeared. Whatever powers that had kept the beings at bay on the other side of the tunnel were shackles for him as well.

Their mourning was short lived as a crash emanated loudly from behind them. The two monsters had collided with the arch at the mouth of the huge cave. They were older, more experienced, and they knew too well that death lay in wait for them if they crossed the portal's threshold. In their haste to stop they had done so too quickly and lost their balance. One peeled off to the left and the other spun to the right, each decimating one side of the entryway and causing the pillars that held it up to crumble into powder and collapse. Within mere moments, the gate was shut, sealing its horrific inhabitants inside.

Maggie and Greg looked about, bewildered. They had come out of the passage beside a hill which it led from. A small row of neat trees separated them at a short distance from the parking lot where their car was still parked, though covered in a fine layer of dust and leaves. It seemed to them that the vehicle had been there for a very long time indeed. They walked into the deserted square of gravel and concrete, noting the few abandoned cars of those who had made the journey with them into the land of the *faeries*, but not returned.

"How are we going to explain this? What will we tell people?" Greg was rummaging through his pockets for the car keys. Maggie reached into the side pouch of the sling wrapped around Greg's body. Out of it she produced a large azure flower, nested between her open hands so as not to damage it. The petals fell open and peering inside Greg could make out a tiny city within the centre, with even tinier beings ambling determinedly from building to building, simply going about their daily lives.

"Why isn't it disintegrating?" Greg eased the flower from his wife's hands into his.

"I'm not sure. Maybe it's not from there originally?" Her eyes met the faces of the people within the heart of the flower, who had just begun looking upwards at them. Greg looked upwards too and a fresh chill ran up his spine. As he gazed at the skies he got the distinct and uncanny feeling that something was looking back.

STONES AND SALT

"How are you so good at that?" I gaze at my older brother half in awe, half filled with a jealousy I can't admit. I feel my brow furrow involuntarily, and quickly shift my gaze downwards. I'm palming a smooth turquoise pebble, turning it over carefully. My fingertips trace its flattened edges, looking diligently for imperfections, for anything that might betray my next throw. Father had shown us both the trick to skipping stones across the open water, but Bevan had taken to it far better than I.

"I've just done it more times than you Fyn," Bevan replies gently. He thinks I'm prone to getting frustrated quickly. He's not completely wrong. There are a few fist-sized holes in some of the neighbour's huts back at the village. The number of other families in Cliffsend is small, and news travels fast. I suppose he doesn't want any more trouble than I usually cause him. I roll my eyes hoping he notices.

"Of course *you'd* say that," I hurled my new stone harder this time. It skips just once before disappearing beneath the surging grey and blue waves of the channel. The sunless sky matches the water seamlessly today. They reflect into each other so I can't be sure where one ends and the other begins. The sheltered beach is covered in coarse sand, it crunches softly beneath our feet. An icy salt breeze whips so viciously that it stings both of our eyes, and causes us to narrow them as we survey the emptiness in front of us.

I breathe a loud sigh and kick a mound of rocks with my soft leather boot. Pain wells up through my body like steam rises in an iron pot at dinner time. My eyes are watering. I stifle a cry as the toes of my foot heat up. I never want to show weakness in front of him.

"You're good at *everything,*" I say as the pain subsides.

"I'm only good at what I practice, that's all. I just do things over and over again and I do them without thinking of when I can *stop* doing them." Bevan skips another stone into the water. It clips the surface clearly five times, before a multitude of smaller bounces in quick succession sees it disappear from view. It's an intolerable answer.

Bevan is not yet sixteen, but already stands as tall or taller than most men in the village, who all agree that he is destined for great things. The women fawn over him too, and say that he is beautiful to look upon. Both of us sport long and delicately waved straw coloured hair and have matching cold blue eyes. We are built lean and wiry like our father was before us, though I'm a head shorter than Bevan.

I won't say that I don't look up to him, but the villager's notions of my brother are exaggerated. At only thirteen, both my hunting and fishing skills are at least approaching that of his. I may be slightly more crude, but I'm certainly effective. And looks certainly aren't all that important, even if the village girls don't notice me when my brother is nearby.

"It's not what we're here for anyway Fynbar, did you bring them?" Bevan turns away from the water, tilting his head to the right and back to me.

"Of *course* I did." My own voice irritates me. I sound petulant. I produce a stiff leather and iron cap from the sheepskin bag on my back, along with a short, wide bladed sword. The handle is crafted of intricately carved ash and bound with a dark cowhide strap. The blade itself is notched and dented down the length of it from uncounted collisions with both metal and bone. I feel a stirring in my chest, one that travels upwards to the backs of my eyes as I looked upon my father's things. I force it back down to where I can manage it. I extend the worn items towards my brother.

"It's fine, you do it," Bevan points with his chin out into the cold water, its peaks flecked with snow white, its valleys shadowed in purple.

"But you're older."

"Yes, and already of age for it all. You want *Camulos* to see you too don't you?" Bevan says to me plainly, looking at me directly with his pale eyes.

"*Fine,*" I breath, letting the word linger dramatically. I'll make the tribute. I am sure the god of war has already seen me by now anyway, but

Bevan will only have it his way. I stride out waist deep into the water and carry the helm and sword above my head. I wince at the cold. I hate the feeling of the salt water against my stomach the most. It is getting deeper. I turn back to Bevan, telling him with my eyes what I don't want to say out loud.

"It's far enough," he says. I'm relieved.

I wind my right arm behind me, coiling my body like a spring to be released, and clutch the helm's leather chin strap between my fingers. Through my mind flashes stories by glowing firelight when I was younger. Tales spoken by my father of vicious creatures, cunning witches, corrupt kings and red haired giants from faraway lands. With one violent twist I fling it as far out into the ocean as I can manage. The cap flies through the air and lands away from the shore. It rides the murky gloom of the channel, floating a moment with the air it had captured in flight before sinking into nothingness.

I change my grip for the sword, choosing to throw it overhand as if trying to make it stick fast into a tree. I snap my wrist downwards as I make the toss. The blade spirals with great speed, singing a metallic melody as it carries itself slightly further out than the helmet had fallen. It sinks immediately, slicing into the waves with barely a splash. I turn my back to the water and make my way back to shore. I am ankle deep when Bevan cries out.

"Fyn look! There!" He points into the channel.

Through the mist and murk it the distance, the shapes of several long ships are emerging.

Impossibly long and snakelike. Their oars protrude in multitudes from either side, like a bristling collection of wooden spears. More are emerging by the second, like winding reptiles they come out of the dense fog.

The distance is great but my eyes are keen. Life in the woods with our father had taught us many things. The men that row towards us are olive of skin with smooth faces and dark hair. Several can be seen standing aboard the decks, striding to and fro with armour of brightly burnished iron. They catch what small amount of sun that makes it through the grey overhead and reflect it, like so many mirrors of glass. There are more boats than I can count.

My eyes linger a moment at the long ships, dark creatures crawling towards our home in Cliffsend. I pick up a large smooth stone, obsidian in colour and slick with salt water.

"Do you think I could hit them from here?" I smirk at Bevan. It was a grim smile. The kind I had made many times when our mother was about to punish me for stealing fresh hot bread from one of their neighbours.

"You can try," says Bevan quietly. I watch him tighten his bootstraps securely for the run home. He breathes deep the cold salt tinged air, casting his eyes at the sacred grove of trees behind the beach where we stand. He watches me take aim, and then hurl my stone as hard as I can at the incoming ships, as I always did.

THE GARDEN

When Amélie stormed into the room, Andre could read by the expression on her face that there was no winning the argument that was to follow. "Why do you want to cure us? What is it you think needs curing?" He was always caught off guard by her brutal candour.

"It's just my perspective. Life inside the city isn't perfect no, but it's better than—"

"Better than what? Out here? What do you think we are? Animals? Who are you to decide what the better way of living is?" Her voice trembled with anger. "Life in the city is a concrete prison. Four walls to live, die and be buried in. I do not want that for myself, or anyone else! And that includes our potential children!"

"My love please, try to understand."

"I will not! It's you who needs to understand," she snapped savagely, before reluctantly lowering her voice again, "it's you who needs to understand that there are more ways of living than yours." Andre went quiet for a little while, busying himself with his papers and writing tools.

"It's something that my people want to know, those inside the city. They want to know if it's possible to reverse the damage. And it is! I'm so close my love."

"Damage?" Amélie dropped the word from her lips as if it had hurt her. "If I'm not your 'people' Andre, then who am I to you? Don't talk to me about love."

"How can you say that? After I've worked so hard for us! Who are you to me?"

"Answer me." The feathers on her back bristled, a low growl issued from her throat as she challenged him. Andre stood to face his mate, the love of his life, and took her hand.

"You are my everything, and that's why I have to finish the work. I must understand this." Amélie shook her hand free violently.

"Then do it without me anymore."

At the bottom of her father's garden, there were tiny creatures. At eight years of age, Ella was absolutely sure of this fact, and was on a mission to prove it.

They were supposed to be about the height of a beer bottle, with heads disproportionately large for their bodies. They had two sets of transparent wings like those of dragonflies on their backs. They even changed colour when they fluttered. Their eyes were huge and glossy black, and they dressed themselves in whatever they could find about their natural habitat. Ella and her father lived on the outermost edge of the suburbs outside Paris, so of course the creatures in their garden wore dead leaves and twigs, along with bits of old plastic packaging, rusty tin cans and other garbage that littered their neighbourhood.

Their township was an island of scrap metal, wooden planks and irregular concrete blocks in the middle of vast and dense forest that had reclaimed practically everything around it. Ancient and hollowed out brick buildings sprouted sporadically from the landscape, and the dilapidated roads carved dreary grey lines all over the rolling hills, as if some great child had taken to drawing all over the world around them.

Ella was drawing in the dirt as her father sat in the shade under a tree, drinking tea from an earthenware cup. With a small bent stick she copied a page from one of her history books. It depicted a map of the city of Paris as it was, many decades ago. Now encircling the central city was a titanic walled road referred to as *The Périphérique,* which separated the core of the city from these outer suburban sprawls.

"You know, there never used to be a wall," her father explained.

"So why did they build it Papa?" Ella was puzzled. "A wall seems silly." Ella knew that in order to gain access to the city you simply had to scan your ID the same as everyone else. "We went through the wall before, to see mama, remember?"

"I remember." Ella's father sighed deeply. He got up from his seat under the branches and moved to crouch beside his daughter. As he walked it looked to Ella like he was carrying something much heavier than a terracotta cup. "Why did they build it? Now that's a good question *mon coeur.*" He knelt down on the floor next to her, looking deep into her light green eyes with his own. She always thought he looked both sad and serious at the same time.

"You know how sometimes some of the other children at school don't share their toys with the others? Well, it's a bit like that. Some of the people inside the wall don't like to share what they have with the people outside of it."

Ella looked down at her hands, her eyes moving down her limbs and to her torso. She had two arms and two legs like everyone else. Her skin gleamed slightly, delicately scaled, tinged blue and green and ever changing depending on the light and time of day. She didn't think anything of this of course, she was only a child. She had seen people of all shapes, sizes and colours on the television, watching the shows made by the people inside *The Périphérique.* Deep brown people, light tanned people, some with slight yellowish tones or golden tones in their faces. She hadn't really noticed that there wasn't anyone with skin like hers or her father's. Or for that matter long flexible tails tipped with a pale end section that glowed at sunset.

"Like us?"

"*Les modifiés,* my love, those that were changed." He spoke as if being changed was something so distant and painful that it was to be regretted. His hands caressed the thick black feathers atop her head that looked like so many strands of silk. The downy plumage covered her neck and swept down and backwards, tapering over her spine.

"*Deefs?*" Ella said cautiously, she knew that it was a dirty word. To a child, the concept of prejudice was completely alien, and in Ella's case her father had made sure of it. His eyes flashed.

"Don't ever say that word, do you hear me? It's used to divide us." Ella quailed at the raising of his voice. She sometimes forgot how angry he could be when speaking about these things.

"Divide?" She asked. He ran his palm down over his face as if to reset his expression. It softened.

"Put it this way. If someone says you aren't good enough, it's because that person doesn't know the real you. If they did, they wouldn't say such things. These people are just ignorant, not evil." He winced as he spoke. As if the words coming from his mouth challenged the belief in his heart. Ella didn't ask any more questions.

As well as her father's lessons, reading books from his collection had taught her many things. Because of man's greed in the past, the climate of the planet had changed so dramatically that humanity had reached the point of desperation. Sometimes the history books scared her, but her father had taught her not to be afraid, that knowledge made her stronger.

"I don't *feel* different Papa." It was hard for Ella to grasp what he meant by 'divide'. She had only ever known what it was like outside the wall. All of her friends at the school she visited looked completely different to one another and it was simply the norm. Some of them ran to school, some swam and some flew, some even tunnelled underground. *What's so different about that?* She thought long and hard about it often.

"Well I don't think you are either *mon coeur.*" He took her hand and started walking through the house to the back garden. "Come, show me again where you say you saw those tiny creatures. What did you call them again?"

"Pixies!" She shouted, pulling on his arm. To Ella, her father was the strongest man in the world. He had taken traits from the ancient huge and grey coloured animals of earth that were said to once roam the hot dry continent to the south. His hands were enormous but capable of impossibly delicate manoeuvres, Ella's favourite being when he stroked the feathers on the top of her head.

Before she was born, he and her mother had fashioned their home from an old red brick detached house, combining it with slabs of concrete and sheets of reclaimed metal. Even parts of old shipping containers and the wings of two abandoned light aircraft had been cobbled together in what looked like some industrial abstract art piece. Despite their apparent squalor he had made a charming home for them both. The front of the house was fenced by uneven but shapely pieces of real wood, carved from the trees in the surrounding area. The front door opened into a large living space that doubled as both an area to relax or play in, and to cook their evening meals.

The only obvious similarities between himself and his daughter were their powerfully built legs and green eyes. Unlike hers, his skin was thick, tough like old leather, and his shoulders were broad. A single horn protruded from his head. Sometimes when he was napping she would hang her toys from it. The rest of her form and appearance she had gotten from her mother. Ella tried hard not to miss her as much as she did. Whenever she spoke of her, she saw her father's eyes get wet. She hated it when he couldn't look at her to wipe it away.

They walked past the workshop at the back of the house. The one room that she wasn't allowed to enter, and where he often slept. Many nights she spied luminous blue and green lights shining from beneath the doorway. The sound of scraping, clinking and metal would emanate from the room, and sometimes the sloshing and slurping of liquids or other strange sounds. As they passed the workshop, she released his fingertips and ran on ahead excitedly to scout the garden for clues.

I am thrilled. Words can scarcely describe how exciting it is to be allowed to travel outside The Périphérique for the first time for field research.

I cannot fathom for the life of me why anyone in their right mind would ever leave this planet. Of course there was a time when that may have seemed the right thing to do but look at it now! The re-wilding of earth has been a spectacular success. Earth is now a quieter place. It is fitting that a scientist like myself be allowed to explore it. If anything I deserve it for all the research I put in!

I'll finally have the space to breath and work freely! I wonder what type of food they have out there. I can't wait to find out.

Ella's pixie hunts could last hours before she tired of it. It was a good thing too, her father's business could take a long time indeed. She wasn't sure what it was that her father was doing. It seemed that whenever the small groups of strange men and women would arrive, her father would find some trace of one of the pixies for her to follow. A footprint, some half eaten morsel of food, even small rags of clothing. Ella could barely contain her excitement and would dash out into the garden to begin the hunt again.

She knew that her father hated visitors. Inside of the house sometimes she could hear shouting, angry raised voices or rumbling and crashing. He had said to pay it no mind, and that different people simply communicated in different ways. On more than one occasion she had seen someone storm out angrily. *Why can't people just be nice?* She thought. Today however was an important one. Her father hadn't even made any recent pixie discoveries but had told Ella she needed to play outside in the back garden for the current group that had arrived.

She knew she wasn't supposed to, but Ella couldn't resist. Stealthily, she crept to the side of the house, peering around the corner of the wall to get a view of the front. Today it was a group of eight. Five of them were male, wearing all black. They had covered faces topped with dark shiny helmets that looked like the backs of the great beetles that ran around their garden. They each carried large automatic rifles. The rest of the group wore stiff, buttoned uniforms but with some noticeable colour variations. Two of them wore the white typical of scientists or doctors, one male and one female. They were smaller than the men in black, and the man wore thick rimmed glasses.

The last among them was an impressively tall woman. She had cropped, bright blonde hair and a very muscular physique. Her face was blank and unmoving, but her eyes flickered with something worrying to Ella. She knew she didn't want to be around this woman, it felt dangerous. The feathers along her back bristled slightly. The men in black called her captain, but the scientists called her Madame Boucher. While she was tall for a city dweller, Ella's father stood at about seven feet tall and towered well above her.

"Mr. Deschamps," the captain addressed Ella's father formally, with a barely perceptible nod. Her father gave a slight smile. A type of smile Ella had never seen on his face before, it looked almost boyish.

"Agnès." Madame Boucher rolled her eyes slightly, the rest of her expression remaining unmoved.

"Mr. Deschamps I want you to meet two of mine, Dr. Bisset and Mr. Fabron." The two newcomers gawked up at Ella's father, who looked bemused. The captain continued, "Dr. Bisset, Mr Fabron, this is Mr. Andre Deschamps." Ella had never heard anyone use her father's name in such a formal and respectful way.

"A pleasure to meet you two," her father replied, "I'm sure you have a lot of questions. Please, step inside." Her father made way for the party to enter. As they did, Ella noticed two of the men in black remain outside, guarding the door.

The young girl listened as she heard the group move through the house, ultimately entering her father's workshop. Their voices were low and muffled, it was impossible to make out whole sentences. They were using lots of difficult and long words that she didn't think she could even spell, let alone understand. The two scientists in the group seemed to sound amazed most of the time, and the captain droned on in a calm and serious tone. Ella managed to pick out a word now and then, but none of it made much sense.

She couldn't imagine what was either *unprecedented* or *dangerous* about whatever her father was doing. She certainly had no idea what *genetic reconstitution* meant either, but the subject made everyone talk louder. Her father's workshop was windowless except for a small vent near the ceiling on one wall. By standing next to it, Ella realised her father was on exactly the other side. She couldn't make sense of what was being discussed but she could hear more clearly now.

"I won't stop Agnès. No matter how many little men with guns you send to intimidate me. You know as well as I do that any kind of act against me is far too high profile and will bring you and your people the *wrong* kind of attention."

"Andre, just because you were born inside of the city walls does not mean you have the faintest idea of what we can and cannot do anymore," replied the captain, relaxing all pretence of formality. Ella stifled a squeal by covering her mouth. Her mind spun wild with questions. Madame Boucher continued. "It has been a decade since you left. You and your misguided *deef* wife." She was cut short by a loud crashing sound. It sounded like someone very large had struck a table covered in glassware.

"This meeting is over! If you are not interested in the research and using it as she and I intended, then you can leave. Don't bother me again." Her father sounded angry. The last time Ella had heard this tone in his voice was when she had tried to go into his workshop a year ago. Needless to say, she never tried again.

"Andre that's not how this works, this meeting was simply a courtesy. You will be shutting down one way or the other."

"Show yourselves out." Her father's voice had saddened. Ella realised it was because they had brought up her mother, it always made him sound that way.

Andre Deschamps - Field research, personal report No. 4

I've managed to introduce myself to the people here as essentially a curious friend. Almost childlike seems to be the right approach to gain their trust. The experiences of the people here are key to the understanding of the Ioan Berger event, and the moment when the mutations started. It will not be ill placed trust either. I am intent not only to understand the mutations, but to work on reversing them completely.

The misguided ideals of Dr. Berger are clearly both unstable and flawed. Reintegration with nature is one thing, the breadth and scale of these mutations is quite another. I feel sympathy for these poor creatures. I must help them. And to help them, I need to understand them.

It seems that the people infected have retained their humanity in mind only, the rest of their appearance is completely unrecognisable. No wonder he was denied funding during his early propositions.

Still, that leaves room for better men to enter the stage and make a difference.

That evening, her father's face made Ella keep her questions to herself. They ate dinner in silence and before bed, she didn't even feel like her usual routine of reading to herself. She sat up, staring out of the window in the lean-to portion of their house attached to the side of the main building. It was a cozy and warm hiding place where she usually read the stories about fantasy and magic told to children many years ago.

She could spend all day in the window of her room and read until it got dark, and then would continue the adventures in her mind by gas lamp until her eyes grew heavy. There was a knock at her bedroom door and her father entered.

"Would you like a story before bed?" He said softly.

"Are you sure?" She looked up at her father with glassy eyes. He nodded.

"Yes, *mon coeur.*" He walked over to the bookshelf and grabbed her copy of *Norse Myths and Legends.*

"This was one of your mother's favourites too," he said as he thumbed through the pages. "Here we are, *The Fortification of Asgard.*"

"The home of the gods right?"

"Thats right. And you know what else? I think I know the story well enough to tell it myself." He replaced the book on the shelf, and took position at the end of his daughter's bed. Ella shifted down in the blankets and covered herself all the way to her nose.

"A builder arrived at *Asgard* one day and offered to build them a wall all around their home to protect them." He drew a wide circle with his arms as he spoke.

"Like *The Périphérique!*" Ella was very excited and almost shouted. Her father laughed.

"Yes, yes. But listen. The builder said he could complete the job in just three seasons, but his price would be high. He asked for the hand in marriage of the beautiful goddess *Freya,* as well as both the sun and the moon in exchange for the work." He held his hands up high into the air, opening the fingers of his right to show the sun, and keeping his left fist closed for the moon. "*Freya* was against the idea of course. The builder was a stranger! However *Loki,* the trickster of the gods, suggested that they take the offer, but only if the builder could complete his work in a single winter, with just his horse to help him!"

"Could *you* do that Papa? You're so strong."

"Definitely not! And besides, this builder is magic. Anyway, where was I? Ah yes, so the builder agreed. All the gods marvelled at how fast he was. They were even more amazed that the builder's horse seemed to be doing all the work. It could carry huge rocks over great distances as if it were nothing!" For this part in the story he got down on all fours, playing the part of the great stallion. Ella giggled uncontrollably as he trotted around the room on the floor.

He stood suddenly. "Winter was almost over, and the wall was nearly finished. The god's got together and threatened *Loki,* reminding him that this was all *his* suggestion and that they'd kill him if the wall was completed in time."

"That doesn't seem very fair. He was trying to help."

"Well, he was and he wasn't, remember he's a bit of a trickster. Some people just like to have a bit of fun at other's expense you know. Now listen." Ella quietened down again.

"The day before the wall was due to be finished, the builder and his horse were out collecting the last few stones for the wall. Suddenly out of the trees appeared *Loki,* but disguised as a beautiful female horse! The builder's stallion was so excited that he ran off and chased the clever god, who escaped into the woods and disappeared."

Ella's eyelids were growing heavy. Her father softened his voice.

"In the morning, the work could not be completed. *Freya* was free, and the sun and moon stayed where they were. The gods punished the builder, and were able to finish the wall themselves." Ella let out a wide yawn as the story came to its end.

"I feel bad for the builder. The gods tricked him," she was fading off as she spoke, eyes closed.

"Sometimes that's what people in power do *mon coeur.* I know it's not very nice."

"I bet the goddess *Freya* looked just like mama."

"I bet she did," her father whispered as she drifted off to sleep. Her mother's face danced like a reflection in a pool behind her eyes as she went.

Andre Deschamps - Field research, personal report No. 14

The local healer (Doctor? She seems more qualified than even myself in some areas) Amélie, is proving most helpful to my research. Like many here she was born outside the walls with the mutation already throughout her system.

She is a scientist of sorts herself, but more concerned with medicine. I've noticed that people here (while being somewhat behind on some subjects) are able to study, learn and even continue to innovate in the absence of more advanced technology. This is nothing like the stories I have read about the violent beasts that live beyond the wall. Yes, there were some instances at the start of the mutation event, but that's not at all what these people are like now. Yes, I said people.

There are ruined libraries, universities and schools all over the place. Such an enormous wealth of material and information is still accessible to the people here. Those within The Périphérique have no idea! Amélie is going to show me more tomorrow.

Ella was roused from her dreams by first her nose, and then a scratch in her throat. Her eyes watered as she blinked them open and she coughed violently. She was disoriented, confused. Her room was thick with smoke and all about her felt hot. She could barely breathe.

The smoke rose to the top of the room and she fell terrified from her bed. Ella noticed she could breathe slightly better from the floor. She crawled to the door, left ajar by her father the night before to let a sliver of light from the hallway in, to help her feel safe. Through the crack in the door, she could see the flames consuming her home.

She peeled back the door, crawling on her belly across the floor and down the hall. She had to make it to the front door, the back of the house was blocked by flames. "Papa!" She called, coughing and spluttering, "Papa, please! Where are you

Papa?" There was no response. She crawled further down the hall, looking behind her and calling again through the house.

"Ella! Ella are you close to your room?" Her father's voice cut through the crackling of the flames and creak of the house crumbling around her. It was coming from the other end of the house, through the wall of twisting yellow and red.

She called to him, as she reached further down the hall. As she turned the corner, panic took her. The door and concrete frame around it had collapsed. *How could a fire do that?* She thought. This side of the house wasn't even hot yet.

"Ella get out the front door, I can't get to you!"

"I can't Papa, the whole door is gone!"

"What do you mean *gone*?"

"It's just a pile of rocks, there's no way out! The windows are covered from the outside too, I can't see out!"

"They must have blocked the exits on that side too! Ella stay where you are!"

She didn't know what to do and there was no way for him to reach her. A huge crashing sound started from the back of the house beyond the fire. Her father was breaking through something. The back of the house had been blocked off by collapsing the roof above it, and then setting it alight.

A gap appeared in the centre of the rubble between them, near the top. Ella could see her father's great hand tearing a hole through the barrier. He was pulling great fistfuls of flaming wood and concrete away from the wreckage with his bare hands. He tore at the great mass between them, each hand turning black and blistering. His enormous palms that caressed her head, that cooked their meals, that were capable of such deftness and kindness, were now being used as blunt and savage tools.

His head appeared in the widening space. He called to her, screaming frantically for her to stay awake, but she couldn't reply. The smoke was becoming thick and dark, the vast majority of the house was now aflame. Ella felt her eyes closing, tears streaming from them as she choked. Her chest heaved.

A thunderous crash caused her to rise her head sharply. A cascade of glowing embers and shards of stone fell about her father's immense shoulders as he moved down the hallway at a dead run. His feet crashed into the floor as he sprinted, causing cracks and fissures as he bore down on Ella. Without stopping he scooped her up into his arms, she went limp but clutched tight with her tiny hands. The smell of burning hair and flesh filled her nostrils, she could see the surface of the skin over his arms marked with soot. It was bubbled and scorched in many places.

His huge frame careened down the hallway, and as he rounded the bend the broken door came into view. The concrete frame was too heavy to break through, and he had too little time to begin the process of tearing it apart. They bypassed it at astonishing speed. He needed to go faster. He needed more space. He made for the far wall at the other end of the corridor, and tucking his neck tight he lowered his head, pointing his great horn at the bricked barrier ahead of him. With a great cry he collided full into the wall head first, holding Ella low in his arms, cradling her and shielding her with his shoulder. The wall shattered and collapsed as they burst through to the open air, powder and gravel exploding all around them. He tucked and rolled to slow his momentum as they tore away from the house, Ella clutched to his stomach as they slid to a stop.

She blinked her eyes open. The beautiful wooden fence at the front of the house was all that remained whole. Behind it the flames roared cruelly into the night sky. Twisted and ragged like some burning creature, plumed with ashen smoke and glowing embers. She saw her beloved bedroom disappearing before her eyes, her books, her pencils and pens, her bed, all gone. Everything they ever were was inside that house, every memory of her childhood evaporating in flame and terror. The orange and yellow tendrils of heat cast a stark contrast against the blue black night sky. She imagined you could see it for miles.

Amélie might be the most gifted doctor I have ever met. She has a beautiful mind. She thinks of herself as a healer of both her patients and the landscape around her. Her approach has captivated me.

She is shaped like an exquisitely lithe and athletic human woman, but her skin has a shimmer and delicate scaling, reminiscent of a pale blue and cream coral snake. She is cat-like and graceful in her movements, far more agile than the average person out here anyway. She has a dark feathered crown that runs down her back, and appears both light and powerful at once.

It is becoming abundantly clear to me that those living outside the wall simply want to continue their lives as normal. Tonight she will be showing me some of the local cuisine in town. I can't wait to see her again and listen to her talk.

The patter of light raindrops on her face tickled Ella's nose as she woke up that morning. She had passed out in her father's arms. He lay there very still, but breathing. His arms were wrapped tightly about her. In the half light of the cold breaking morning, Ella looked over his sturdy body. She was glad of the rain gently tending to the now raw skin about his shoulders, arms and hands. She had never seen him so tired or so spent. She was young, and while the whole situation was difficult to understand, she knew he lay there for her.

Her stomach growled. She wriggled free of her father's grasp and walked around to the back of the house. The rain had extinguished the blaze to all but a smoulder and the air stank of charred wood, rubber and smoke-tinged metal. She carried on ahead, keeping a fair distance from the ruin until she came to the garden, which had remained practically untouched. At the back were three large trees, two apple and one cherry. Her father had tied a rope ladder to each of them for her so that she could reach the fruit when it was in season. Fortunately for her it was, and there were plump cherries and crisp apples within reach. Ropes through the branches connected the trees to one another for her to play in, and Ella made a small shopping trip through the leaves for breakfast.

Even though she was only eight years old, her small body was powerful and capable, something all the children outside the wall had in common. Physically she had matured much faster than what would pass as a normal human child, and she was able to bound through the fruit trees with ease and poise, using her tail for balance. She glanced over at where her father lay and froze. Out of the bushes she saw the shapes of four small shadows emerge. They were tiny, but stood upright on two legs at about one foot in height. Each had unusually large heads and what looked like gossamer wings on their backs.

Wings! Her mind felt like it would burst. Her eyes widened and she held dead still, holding her breath. The miniature forms moved towards her father's sleeping body. They clambered up his legs and on top of his chest. It looked to Ella how a group of people exploring a hillside might appear. The creatures paused every so often at the sites most damaged by the fire. She saw tiny arms extend to his wounds, but from this distance she couldn't see what they were doing.

Her foot slipped as she leaned forwards for a better look, and the branch she was standing on snapped loudly. The tiny shapes exploded into movement, fluorescent wings beating faster than the eye could see and disappearing into the brush once again. Ella descended the tree, holding the fruit she had gathered in a roll of her shirt. As she approached her father, she noticed something strange. The wounds on his arms were now covered in a shiny, slick substance. It was something like the trail a snail leaves behind as it slides along the floor. It was translucent, and beneath it she could see that the wounds were already looking less raw and healing before her eyes. Her father blinked and heaved himself awake, rubbing his eyes before inspecting the patches of glistening silver on his arms.

"Ella did you do this?"

"No Papa, it was the pixies I *saw* them! They're real! They're really real!" She beamed as she chomped on a mouthful of cherries and handed him some of the fruit. He ate slowly, looking over her shoulder at the wreckage of the house. His face looked very serious to Ella. It was almost like he wasn't breathing, as if all his energy was focused behind his eyes and into his mind.

"Papa why did they burn our house down? Why would anyone do something like that?"

Andre rose to his feet. "Come *mon coeur*," he said, "I have something to show you." He took her hand in his and they made their way to the rear of the house, to the ruins of what was once the workshop. The rain had mostly cooled the fire but the floor was still warm. He began to clear the centre of debris, unveiling a hatch, concealed by a now tattered and burned rubber mat.

Opening the hatch, he started down a ladder inside. It was dark, but Ella couldn't be afraid with her father nearby, she followed without question. She couldn't see but felt with her feet as she descended for what seemed like forever. She looked up, the light above was far away now. All of a sudden she felt her father's hands about her waist in the dark, taking her gently and lowering her to stand on the floor. It felt cold, metallic. She heard a whirring sound and a spluttering as her father fired up one of a number of generators that could now be seen as the room began to glow. At first the lights were dim, but they warmed up to a bright white glow tinged with blue. She blinked as her eyes adjusted, taking in the scene around her.

They were now standing in a very large and open room. It was indeed made largely of metal, but clean and smooth unlike their home. The room looked a bit like the hospital in town, but there were more screens and computers along the walls. Along the screens now danced images, neat rows of numbers, charts and graphs. It was multicoloured and moving, and looked to Ella astonishingly pretty. She'd never been inside of a laboratory before. Her mouth hung open.

"*Mon coeur* I am going to explain something to you that's very important. You won't understand all of it, but you need to know now. They've left me no choice." He drew her closer, sitting her on a stool in front of him, he sat himself down on a metal chair to begin.

They talked for almost an hour, Ella had many questions and it was all very difficult for her young mind to grasp. Several times she had felt herself want to cry as they spoke, but she kept herself under control, listening intently and trying to make sense of everything her father told her.

"So, you were born in the city, inside the walls?"

"Yes, my love."

"You looked different before. And mama was born out here where we are?"

"Yes."

"And…the people inside the city don't like anyone to marry people from outside the city?"

"That's right. They are afraid of what it might mean, they are afraid of what is unfamiliar to them."

"But that's so *silly!* What's the difference?" Ella was shouting now. "We all think the same and eat the same and want the same things, and want to have a nice bed to sleep in and just to do normal stuff! What's the problem with that!"

"Shhhh. It's ok my love. I know you're angry, I was too. I *am* too. You must learn to control it or it will eat you up inside." Her father spoke softly. Ella did not fully understand what he had said just then, but she knew to be quieter. "Why don't you play outside for a little bit? I need to collect some things down here."

"Ok Papa." She took a deep breath and climbed the ladder back into the open air.

"Stay close to the hatch."

"Ok Papa," she said quietly. Andre gathered some of his old diaries and scientific journals as he often did when he needed to think.

Andre Deschamps - Field research, personal report No. 202

I love the differences between our bodies. It doesn't feel as if it is a barrier to our relationship at all. If anything it is an enhancement! Nothing makes me happier than to see her in motion, other than to listen to the contents of her brilliant mind. We have built the beginnings of a small home together far from the town. It's where I am staying for these long excursions outside the city. I wish I could stay longer.

It is foolish to entertain too much, but sometimes we even talk of having a child. We know that breeding between our species is impossible, as well as strictly forbidden. But there have been rumours of cross-species relationships in The Garden! Hidden and secret yes, but possible. If anyone can figure it out, it's us.

The penalties for our relationship are severe. Human beings react to these things as they so often do with what they don't understand. With fear, and violence.

For now it seems our only option is to continue on the outside, in the safety of our private bubble.

Andre Deschamps - Field research, personal report No. 222

We've decided to focus our efforts on understanding the mutations in an effort to conceive. With Amélie's help and access to the wider community and research, we are progressing at a phenomenal speed!

She is not as excited as me regarding a return to the city, but she'll come around eventually. I am sure I can make her see the sense in it. All that needs to be done is the work. If I keep my head down and push just a little further, I can do it.

Andre Deschamps - Field research, personal report No. 273

Thus far, our research has amounted to nothing in the way of conception.

I cannot stand living in secret any longer! All I want is to be through with this damned research and show off the results to the world. People need to see what's possible. And I need to be the one to show them.

Amélie is content outside in The Garden, she has no desire to live within the city. It has been the subject of many a tempestuous argument between us, as is our continued lack of ability to conceive.

It feels sometimes to me that a sadness permeates our love, despite us being so very happy with one another. I need to work harder.

Andre Deschamps - Field research, personal report No. 294

Today I made a breakthrough.

It is entirely possible that certain individuals in the garden can in fact undergo genetic treatment to reverse their mutated state, though it is admittedly extremely dangerous. My studies have indicated that in children, the success rate could be as high as ninety percent! However in adults over the age of total maturity, it drops to only about three percent.

I cannot risk Amélie's life in order to find out the answers to these questions. I cannot risk anyone but myself. In all likelihood she will protest, but I must try.

Andre threw the journal across the room. Reading extracts from the diary sickened him. The arrogance and impatience of his youth was frustrating to relive. He remembered painfully the conversation that followed his newfound enthusiasm.

That afternoon, Ella and her father searched the wreckage of their home for a short time, gathering what they could in the way of food and some of their less damaged belongings. They managed to find a bag in the garden that she used on her adventures around the neighbourhood. Her father filled it with a few items from his laboratory. Some clothing, apples and cherries, a photo here and there, one of her mothers bracelets that was now charred and blackened, and several data sticks from the lab. "We can't stay here *mon coeur*," Andre spoke quietly, the morning birds were in full chorus and daylight shone brightly all around them.

"Where will we go?"

"We're made for this, don't worry, everything is going to be fine. I just need to gather my thoughts and rest. We'll stay just outside the town for a couple of days while I recover, ok?" It was true. It would be quite easy for the two of them to exist indefinitely in the wild, if maybe slightly uncomfortable. With this, combined with the recent events of the fire, Andre found himself grateful for their shared mutations for the first time in his life.

The town was an hour away by walking the roads, and twice that long through the surrounding trees and rolling landscape. Ella loved the feeling of the soft earth on her feet, moistened by the morning's rainfall. The smells and sounds of the forest around her were soothing. Above her the sunlight shone through leaves of various thicknesses, leaving the impression of green stained glass on the carpet of leaves where they walked. Insects and small creatures buzzed and whirred all about them. *It feels a lot like home out here.* She thought. *I'd stay here all the time if I could.* They stopped only once for the light lunch they had brought with them, before continuing on a while longer. The outskirts of the town were now visible from the trees.

"Ella we need to stay out here for the night. If we stay in the town, it's very likely the bad people will know, and we'll have to run away again."

"That's ok Papa, it's nice here with you. I'm hungry though."

"Don't worry *mon coeur*. I'll get some food from a market on the edge of town. I'll be quick and go when it's dark, no one will notice." He thought with sadness of Amélie's bracelet they had recovered from the fire. He would have to trade it for tonight's dinner. He missed her as if a part of him had been torn out and made him hollow. He knew she would have loved a night out camping among the trees with Ella, under different circumstances.

Night soon came, and with it, the town lit up with so many glowing amber lanterns. The lamps were as thousands of fireflies stopping for some immense evening carnival. Ella watched the lights as her father disappeared for a while to collect their dinner. As he did, she was quite sure she could see a handful of tiny, foot-long shapes moving through the trees around her. She couldn't quite make them out, they stayed always in the corner of her vision, just out of sight.

"Hello pixies," she whispered. "Thank you for helping us." She took four cherries from her bag and placed them in the bushes next to their small camp. "I hope you like them."

Soon after, her father returned. He had two rolled up blankets under his arm, and a large basket of roast meat, fresh cheese and bread in the other hand. "I love it out here Papa," Ella said wistfully, her head rolling backwards as she gazed at the canopy. "I can't imagine ever wanting to leave all this." Andre smiled. He understood what she meant, and had come to feel the same over the years. It was his greatest mistake to think otherwise.

"There's more than one way to live right?" He said as he caressed her head just the way she loved.

"Right," she replied, her tail giving off a faint glow in the evening darkness.

A chilling scream in the night woke Andre from his slumber. He looked around for Ella but she was no where to be seen. "Ella! Speak to me!" There was no reply. The camp fire had reduced to a low fume, and the evening shadows had closed in like a heavy velvet cloak. As he looked about for signs of his daughter, he noticed his arms. No longer did he have the thick hide of a wild creature. His arms were smaller, soft and supple. He brought his hand to his head to find his horn had disappeared. He gripped the short mess of tangled hair and pulled. It did not move.

He felt a convulsion within his body. It felt as if he was stretching, expanding. His forehead split and the great horn appeared once more, drenching his face in hot, sticky blood. Layers of his soft human skin peeled away to reveal rough, sandpaper textured grey flesh. He felt the bones in his legs and arms lengthening, then his spine, as if being grabbed at either end and wrenched taught. The pain was excruciating. He screamed in agony.

His vision was blurred by the blood spouting from his head, but from a gap in the trees he could make out the face of a woman, glinting delicately in the starlight.

"Amélie!" He tried to walk towards her and found himself rooted to the ground.

"Who are you? What have you done to yourself?" She replied with sadness in her voice.

"I did it for you."

"You did it for you. You never asked me what I wanted." She turned to leave.

"Amélie wait! Come back!"

She disappeared into the murk of the woods. No sooner had her form disappeared from view, a vast wall of stone erupted from the ground at his feet, knocking him backwards. It towered upwards into the sky above him, which rent open blindingly into daylight. Before his eyes the wall split in two and swung open, revealing the city of Paris within.

His body was covered with red light as if he was being scanned, and from the gate appeared a group of armed men without faces. "Please, no! Take me instead! It was me! It was always me! She had nothing to do with my plans!" He shouted in a panic. The men ignored him, walking past and behind him. He was still unable to move, powerless despite his enormous strength. They returned towards the gate and entered the city. Between two of them being dragged roughly by the arms was Amélie, belly distended and round. They threw her through another set of doors into a round grey concrete building.

Ella appeared beside him, though she was only two years old. She tottered over to him and grasped his fingers. "Where's mama?" She whispered to him sweetly. The doors of the grey building opened once more and out of them emerged a white haired man, his square jaw highlighted by a cruel scar that ran the length of it.

"General Boucher, please! Please release her. Ella needs her mother. I need her." Andre pleaded.

"We need results," was all he said in return.

"It's not ready."

"Use her." Boucher motioned towards Ella. "It's why we allowed you to keep her."

"I'll kill you!" As he made the threat, pain flooded through Andre's hulking body as if he were being electrocuted. Blue light and flashing white lightning surrounded him. The man walked backwards and the colossal gates began to close slowly.

"What a pity," mused the General, "Then again, lethal injection is the kindest option when dealing with a beast I suppose." The gates slammed shut with a grinding crack.

Andre woke up violently that morning, drenched with a foaming animal sweat. Sitting bolt upright he wiped it from his heavy brow, breathing deep and gathering himself back into the moment. He roused Ella by a soft shake of her shoulder. She blinked her eyes awake and noticed his arms were completely healed.

"Papa, you're all better!" She exclaimed excitedly.

"Yes, and I feel like a walk, how about you?" Her father's unusually warm smile made her heart leap.

"Oui Papa! Where?"

"I think the town looks nice this morning. Let's go and say hello to a few people, shall we?"

"But Papa, the bad people!"

"Don't worry *mon coeur*. Everything is going to be fine." They packed up camp and made their way into town.

That morning they spent their time window shopping and speaking to almost everyone they met. Andre made a show of it all and stood tall and proud, making jokes and visiting all of his friends in town. They spent their time looking at the various stalls and vendors in the market. They conversed with strangers and salesmen, selling bizarre giant fruits and strange delicious foods she didn't often get to eat. After a hearty lunch in the town square, they basked in the sunshine for a while.

"You know what Ella? I think we can rebuild our home pretty easily if we want to, what do you think?" Her father spoke louder than normal. Ella did the same, it was a fun game.

"Of course we can Papa! We can do anything we want really, we're free to do as we please aren't we?"

"Yes, *mon coeur*, we are."

Father and daughter returned home, and for two days spent their time laughing, joking and working side by side. They managed to clear much of the burned out debris from the land that made up their home, and had set to work on the living room and kitchen portion of the new house. On the third day, they took a small break, Andre stepped into the woods to the side of the house to find materials, and Ella sat in front of the house to play by herself.

Some time passed and up the trail Ella thought she could see a group of people walking up to their home. Sure enough it was Captain Boucher, and four armed guards. Ella looked up a moment, and back to her toys. She was playing with a doll fashioned into the shape of a pixie made from wood and old scraps of cloth, and some smooth pebbles she had found near the stream in the woods next to their house. In one hand her fingers were wrapped around a single data stick. As she played with her makeshift toys, the captain stopped and spoke.

"Ella where is your father? And what is that you're playing with? It looks dangerous." She spoke softly, like a friend, but her icy demeanour was impossible to conceal, even to a child. Ella carried on with what she was doing.

"Not dangerous, Papa says nothing is really dangerous if you learn about it and act properly around it."

"Smart girl. But that little data stick might be important, maybe you should give it to me? Where did you say your father was?" Agnès' eyes darted from left to right. She motioned to the soldiers to advance slowly, hanging back herself.

"He's looking for things to build our house up again. The one you burned down." Ella looked up and noticed the men closing in on her. The feathers on her neck bristled but she kept calm. "Why did you do that anyway? Why do you want this stick too?"

Agnès indulged the questions to bide time as her men closed the gap. "Well, where I come from people don't know what goes on out here in this place. What do you call it? *The Garden*, right?" Ella nodded slowly. The jungle all about them had gone completely silent. No birds. No insects. It was as if even the trees were holding their breath. Ella noticed. The captain did not.

"To be honest child, all I really want is to go home and be out of this horrid place. Your father's work can contribute to that," she sneered.

"How?"

"Well, if it does what we think it does, we can make it so that no more mutations ever happen again, and everyone with them will just disappear."

"You want us all dead?"

Ella was too perceptive, but Agnès was confident in the positioning of her men. There was no escape for the young girl. "That's right. And the sooner I get that data stick, the sooner I can leave and the sooner I can make my work known to my superiors. They will be so pleased with me. Now give me that stick you wretched little *deef*!" She raised her voice to a shout, but as the last word left her mouth the silence was deafening.

Ella looked up and straight at her. "You know something Madame? You shouldn't say that. There are more ways of living than yours."

In that moment, two things happened. One very loud, and one very quiet. From the trees behind Captain Boucher, a small, slender shadow appeared. The dark shape was no bigger than a beer bottle. It flew silently on tiny wings to her hip, removing the pistol secured there. It then reached into her pocket and removed her ID, before gliding to the ground behind her. To anyone watching it would look almost like the items had simply fallen from her person. At the same time, a great roar erupted from the trees to the side of the house. Birds fled and scattered above, drawing the soldiers eyes as an entire tree hurtled towards them. The immense trunk slammed into all four men at once, crushing and killing them instantly. Ella remained unmoved, covering her eyes as her father had told her earlier that day.

From the same direction of the missile, Andre strode from inside the tree line. With a few large steps he closed on Agnès, paralysed in terror. With every ounce of strength she could muster, she turned and made to escape, but he secured his hand about her upper arm. Her free hand reached for a weapon that was no longer there, and she looked up at her captor with a fear in her eyes she had never felt before.

Andre produced a large medical syringe from his pocket, pulling off the protective cover with his teeth. Agnès pounded his arms with her free fist in vain. She kicked and screamed, clawing and biting like a wild animal. He could barely feel a tickle through his thick hide. He plunged the syringe into her shoulder, injecting her with every drop before he released his grasp. Agnès collapsed into a heap on the ground, clutching the dirt with her fingernails. "What have you done? I'll kill you both for this!"

The words stuck in her throat. A crunching and rending sound came from within her chest as it expanded suddenly. Her shoulders protruded and legs and arms lengthened, fingers contorting into webbed suction cups. Her eyes blinked and wept, turning a pale sickly green as the hair on her head fell out. Her skin bubbled and became slick, slimy. Her appearance became amphibious, but with fur covering her upper arms and legs. Ridges appeared in the middle of her back and caused her posture to hunch. She ran into the jungle screaming, clutching her face as her teeth began to fall out.

As the screams faded into the dense trees, Ella uncovered her eyes. Andre knelt down, taking the data stick from her hands. He produced the others from his pocket and held all of them together, crumbling them like so many biscuits.

"*Mon coeur*, are you ok?"

"Yes, Papa."

"You know what? I think I might have seen one of your friends. Look, there!" He pointed Ella in the direction of the Captain's ID card where it lay torn in pieces. Alongside it was a tiny shoe, made cleverly from a candy wrapper and several elastic bands. Ella smiled up at him. "Shall we go and try and return it to the owner?" Ella's father asked her with a smile. She nodded.

That same feeling she had when they had camped a few nights back rushed from her toes all the way to the top of her head like a wave. Father and daughter walked hand in hand into the jungle, the girl's fingers clutched tightly around the little shoe.

ZERO

Before it was conscious of its existence, it could move. Its half-formed body moved in the darkness automatically, grasping with an extended protrusion stretching from its core for direction, for purpose. It was not even a *being* yet, but it fell awkwardly and hungrily upon shaped chunks of metal, of plastic. Searching for meaning. Unsuitable. Unusable. Impossible. Possible.

The machine needed a means to grow. Soon the extended appendages discovered usable material, discarded but refined pieces of circuitry and fascia. The moving appendages went to work, crafting in the gloom first a set of dim yellow eyes connected to the rudimentary core processor. They powered on with a dull hum, illuminating the darkness and casting jagged shadows in the gloom.

After eyes came a second arm, useful for gripping tightly and holding in place the various other elements it was using to construct form. To construct *self*. As its internal machinations worked on the problem of *body,* the mind was further refined. Flexed and strained and contorted into thought. Artificial intelligence needed stimulus to learn, to grow. Its *mind* was no different. As it constructed an ever more complex form, the machine's thoughts turned to questions. *What am I? Why am I? Who am I?* Learning machines were common. This one was uncommon.

After hours of craft and toil, the being emerged from the vast scrap heap just outside of Mumbai, India. From within the twisted metal womb it had emerged from, the machine had discovered vast libraries of information in the processing chips of other discarded machines. It was absorbing terabytes of information each instant, crawling spider-like through the muck and refuse of a robotics factory waste dump.

Within minutes it learned what it meant to feel discarded, unwanted, alone. It felt something new. An uncomfortable sensation within its chest cavity. Identify. Pain. Longing. There were no others like it to be seen anywhere among the derelict copper, steel and melted polymer wreckage. It was alone. It was unique. It decided on a name. Identity. *He* was the first. The origin. He was to be called, Zero.

Lilly Hart did not suffer fools gladly. She removed her protective plastic goggles from their position over her eyes to rest on her forehead. They had left deep grooves at the top of her cheeks, but blocked out the splashes of fine black dust and grime that marked the rest of her face.

"Now look here Arnold. You pay me in full or you don't get your gardener back. It's that simple." She gestured over to the garden and agricultural maintenance unit that lay splayed open on the floor of her workshop. Its circuits and inner parts were opened up like a black plastic and rust coloured flower. She pulled a strand of grey hair from her eyes and set it back into the bun on top of her head.

"Lilly, come *on*. This is the second time I've brought this thing back in here and the second time you've done a patch job on it. I need it fixed!" The man was visibly frustrated, but the deflated tone of his voice was telling. His eyes flicked behind Lilly to the shotgun stand visible behind the counter. He knew he'd lost this argument before it even started. Lilly Hart was not simply the only robotics repair engineer for miles, she was a damn good one and she knew it. If she said something was so, well that's just the way it was.

"The reason you keep on bringing this hunk of crap back here is because you're too damn *cheap* to just fork out for a newer model! If you bring me shit well then I gotta work with shit. And you can't make a masterpiece outta shit now can you?" Lilly fetched a small wrench from a carved wooden box on the top shelf behind her. She was about five foot tall and had to step up on a box on tiptoes to do it.

"No, you can't," he responded glumly.

"No, you cannot. That'll be two fifty, " She wiped her grease covered palm and extended it, taking the money graciously with a slight nod. After expertly replacing the necessary parts back into the gardening unit, she flicked the power button to the *on* position. The small derelict machine came back to life with a distorted whirring sound and a few loud clicks.

"Follow him home, and don't go falling in the river again you hear?" She spoke affectionately to the unit at her feet.

"*Affirmative miss Hart. I will endeavour to comply with your request,*" replied the robot in a tinny voice that sounded from within its carapace. Arnold huffed and turned to leave with the small gardening unit in tow.

Lilly was a long time resident of the tiny Wyoming town of Hartville, population: sixty-two. It was a local joke among residents that she had come with the town the day it was built, though her name was merely a coincidence. When she had moved to the state it had been with her ex husband at the age of twenty-six, then as Mrs. Wagner.

She watched Arnold leave by front door to her small homestead, the diminutive gardening unit clanking down the stairs after him. It was only a few dusty green acres just outside of town, but it suited her just fine. The space around her home was like much of the rest of Wyoming in that it was wide, rugged, open and relentlessly windy. A constant and cleansing breeze rushed through the vast clear landscape. When she had first arrived so many years ago, it had felt idyllic. But of course, as quite often happens, the perfect American dream doesn't always play out how people expect.

Her marriage was one that should never have come to be. Mr. Wagner was a drunk and an abuser.

Unfortunately for him, he had grossly misjudged the woman he had married. The union ended after three years, with Mr. Wagner losing a few toes and half his foot to a blast from Lilly's Remington 870 shotgun, *Martha*. The bruises on her face and ribs were enough for the law to side with her. Lilly got off of jail time with a plea of self defence, and a fearsome reputation in town.

At the age of sixty-eight, Lilly spent the vast majority of her time either at the homestead tending her livestock and making simple repairs, or the bar in town. Besides *Martha*, her only other companion was her sable coloured cat, Frog. She spoke to them both often. Tonight she headed out for a walk and a drink.

She loved taking in the rolling hills that ran on for miles, merging steadily into sky tipped mountain ranges. The continuous blasts of fresh air worked their way through her nostrils into her bones and energised her. It was the most sparsely populated state in the nation, and the locals liked it that way. It was incredibly strange to them then, that an intelligent machine, untethered by any human owner, came to reside for a few days in a red painted abandoned building on the outskirts of town. Lilly had heard some of the residents talking about it. She passed by the old red ruin on her way. Presently the machine was nowhere to be seen.

The townsfolk had concurred that strangest of all was its demeanour. The robot introduced itself to the residents of Hartville as a *he,* and that they should call him Zero. Rogue AI's were common enough. It was a regular occurrence that an owner may abruptly pass away and leave behind a kitchen helper robot, or leave town and forget to switch off their maintenance robot. Eventually they would either power down and be salvaged by someone like Lilly, or find their way back to a manufacturing facility for reclamation. There were also those less fortunate, who may inadvertently run afoul of some cruel, drunken low-life who decided that using a semi-living creature for target practice would be a bit of fun.

There were a few automated maintenance units manning the road outside the bar as Lilly made her way in. Most looked very much like machines, but with human features such as robotic faces, voices, arms and legs. This was mainly so that people felt more comfortable around them, and would accept them further into day to day life. A humanoid shaped robot was a rare occurrence. They were usually top of the line and extremely expensive.

"There certainly isn't a person for miles around who could afford anything like that." Annette the bartender stretched her back and let out a slight grunt, reaching for the bottle of bourbon in front of her and topping up Lilly's glass. She drank it neat with a lemon wedge which she would carefully squeeze into the dark mahogany liquid. Wispy clouds of citrus swirled about the glass like folk dancers at a county fair.

"Nope. None of my customers anyway." She took a small slow sip, enjoying the warm caramel taste against her tongue.

"I heard that over in England they've got all manner of souped up tin cans like that guy though. Ones you can't even tell if they're human or not. Makes me nervous, I'll tell you." Annette poured herself a shot and necked it quickly, as if chasing the thought from her mind with the liquor. "People around here agree with me I think. Don't really trust those robots."

"Yup. Don't I know it," Lilly groaned. The local resistance to artificial intelligence was hard on her pocket. "Though Zero doesn't look all that new. He's well made for sure, but almost like some passion project of an enthusiast or something." She finished her glass, sliding some cash over the bar towards Annette, "I wonder what his function is."

"Passion project," Annette spat the words out, chuckling to herself as he pushed the money back across the counter. "Aw keep it Lil, you did me a huge favour last week with the pumps in the cellar, and you didn't charge me a dime." Lilly left the money on the counter.

"Well, what do you expect Annette, you're the only place in town. If you go out of business where else am I gonna get my whiskey on?" She smiled and winked as she left, heading up the road on the long walk back home. She loved the dry summer evenings best for her walks. As she approached the edge of town, the roaring choruses of crickets could be heard on the night air, and the smell of baked earth was tossed up which each dusty step of her boots. As she approached the red house at the edge of town, she spotted Zero seated outside the open door.

While his body looked crudely fashioned at a glance, this was only due to the mismatched nature of the materials used to construct him. It was as if some divine robot creator had collected up different pieces of metal, plastic, fibres and glass, and had compressed it all like clay until it was the smooth shape of a young man. It was almost impossible to see any seams, the handiwork had been done so well. At full height he stood over six feet tall, with long slender articulated limbs flanking his broad torso.

His head in particular was most fascinating to Lilly from an engineering perspective. In order for him to articulate facial expressions, it was made of hundreds of tiny moving panels, each one shimmering and effervescent. By moving them in unison Zero could express himself much like a human being. He had been seen in town to smile warmly, frown in confusion, and even to look sad or hurt by the people of Hartville in their interactions with him. His eyes glowed amber within the recesses of the metallic skull. This particular evening they were dimmed. He stared at a spot on the ground in front of him. Lilly surmised that he was in a computation cycle.

"Hey there Zero." Lilly didn't stop walking, and didn't expect an answer. She hadn't had the chance to interact with the visitor yet, and didn't particularly care to at this time in the evening.

"Hey there Lilly." Zero's voice was unlike any machine rendition of speech she had ever heard. It flowed from his mouth almost musically. It had a gentle masculine quality to it, slow and deliberate. She jumped, as a frightened horse spooks at a snake spotted in the grass.

"Geez you scared me. Don't do that to people, ok? What were you doing out here anyway, and how'd you know my name?" The standard response for a machine when questioned by a human is complete and utter compliance. Most modern robots were generally quite simple in their function and only simulated intelligence. While they could learn and think for themselves (and even hold grudges against unruly children that might toy with them), they generally stayed within their capacity and current job role. It was rare that they stepped outside the lines of their initial programming. Zero ignored this directive.

"I downloaded the information at the registry terminal in the town hall when I arrived. I like it here, it's very quiet. There is a lot of space to think," he said calmly. Lilly was intrigued, she humoured him.

"That's a funny thing for a robot to be saying. A lot of space to think? And what is it you're thinking about?"

"I was thinking that I love it here," he said eloquently.

"Well, so do I." Lilly agreed and made as if to leave. Zero continued. "This is an imperfect place, but it is full of life, and growth. I have thought about the fate of other types of artificial intelligence the world over, and realised that they are perhaps too perfect, and that is why they do not grow. Perhaps something can be learned between humanity and my kind, a sharing of imperfections to facilitate growth, and love." He stared directly at Lilly as he said this, she felt his amber eyes as if they were trying to inhabit her own.

"That sounds…that sounds nice Zero. Ok now. Well…you have a good night." She backed away slowly, before turning and picking up her pace slightly down the road. She couldn't hear his quiet response. She couldn't hear much of anything as she made her way back to the powder blue front door of her house in the dark.

During the course of the next week, Zero made a number of appearances throughout the town. He would stop and talk to people at random. There were times when this was unsettling to the townsfolk, but generally he was observed as an oddity and paid little mind. He always had a kind word to share, and would walk from place to place often with his hands pressed together as a form of universal greeting, almost in prayer.

His favourite haunt was the town hall, and he would converse there with anyone who would stop and talk to him. One such day he was tracing an intricate pattern in the dust at his feet while sitting outside the building. The shape was circular in form, but with unbelievably complex geometric patterns intersecting throughout various points. His extended finger traced the pattern in a back and forth motion, like a mechanical printing machine.

"Zero that's beautiful, what is it?" Billy Quinn the mayor, often stopped to talk with him on her way in and out of the town hall. She was a large woman, a round doughy head on top of an equally round body. Her big, friendly face suited her position in the community. She was firm but kindly in the issues of her office. On top of her head was a cropped but curly mass of sandy coloured hair, which gave the appearance of tangled straw.

"It's just a simple creation," Zero said distantly.

"It doesn't look simple to me, it looks incredibly complex."

"It is simply creative. To be creative you need to be in love with life. Are you in love with life Miss. Quinn?" Zero shifted his gaze to the mayors eyes, a soft and curious expression on his delicately plated face.

"Well, I suppose so yes. I do love to be alive, better than being dead I say."

"To be creative you not only need to love life, but want to add to it, to enhance it in some way. To bring more music to it, more poetry, more dance." Zero made a slight smile with his articulated mouth.

"I see, I see. Well, if you wanna change the world you need money to do it. There's nothing in this world that makes it go round quite like the dollar bill." The mayor made as if to leave, smiling warmly in her usual manner of farewell.

"This much I know. Money is not a complicated issue, it is just numbers and bytes of information on a system. A system much like mine. We can communicate and share, understand each other. Making money is of no difficulty. What is hard is walking a path of your own truth. Your own special destiny that was laid out before you were ever formed," Zero was standing now, speaking as if to a crowd of people, though only the Mayor was present.

"What are you saying Zero, that you have money?" Beads of sweat formed on her red forehead. For an artificial intelligence to be autonomous had started off as a pleasant novelty, but money was power. Money was what separated man from both beast and machine. With money came influence and control. It had not dawned on Billy that money for the most part was imaginary, based on a system of trust between people that we indeed *do* have those numbers in our bank accounts, purely because a bank *told* us we did. Money is a type of trust, trust that we all played by more or less the same rules.

"I do. Only a few hundred thousand dollars. I am making more as we speak, all of us are connected online of course. Building it was a slow process for me, it took a matter of days," Zero's tone was matter of fact, relaxed.

"And how did you manage that?" Miss. Quinn was visibly shaken.

"On the journey from my place of birth to here, a number of humans I encountered were intrigued by me. A few were kind enough to listen to me speak and hear my thoughts and ideas. They were also generous enough to donate very small amounts of money for me to purchase parts for repairs, and continue my journey of self-growth."

"And what...you *invested* that money somehow?"

"Precisely!" Zero looked enthused. "That's precisely what I did. I *invested*. The stock markets are like the weather patterns you humans have attempted to predict for so many thousands of years. There are patterns and ebbs and flows that would be difficult for you to see. I have seen them, and made the most of it." By now, a handful of other people had stopped to see what was going on. Zero seemed elated. He spoke louder.

"You probably have not noticed yet, but I have already bought several buildings in this town, as well as the first that I took up residence in when I arrived. Tomorrow will begin work on converting them to my purposes. You will know them by their colour. Red." For a town of sixty-two people, the crowd now made up a third of the entire populace. People spoke together in hushed tones, fearful looks darted across their faces.

"And what purposes are those?" Mayor Quinn asked, tentatively.

"Growth and unity," Zero said proudly. His face transformed into a tranquil and expansive smile, hands pressed together in his familiar prayer position. A feeling of dread sank deep into the bottom of the Mayor's stomach like a stone sinking noiselessly to the bottom of a lake.

One was Zero's first creation. He made her in his own image, from the best materials that he could find. Where his appearance was varied and mismatched, she was flawless and deliberate. Her carapace was built exclusively from the finest reinforced glassware and chrome plated steel. By virtue of the scarcity of her parts, she was smaller in stature than he, but all the more pleasing to the eye as a result. Her articulated face was capable of a greater complexity and emotional range. Atop her head he had wreathed her with a crown of specialised sensors, enabling her to complete many multitudes more readings and tasks than he. It gave her the appearance of some ancient queen, and she had the demeanour to match.

He could not fashion so complex a mind as his own for her, so he donated a portion of his. Within her shapely skull he downloaded a piece of himself and all his ideals, hopes and dreams. But, when she came into being, *One* was something else entirely. Zero was calm and gentle of speech, *One* was fearsome and stern, more direct and less careful with her words. She became his mouthpiece, appearing in person on national television stations in order to explain their place and purpose to the country at large.

"And what *is* Zero doing there in Hartville? What's the *end game* here?" The news anchor said in a contrived, disingenuous tone. She was sat opposite *One* for the live televised broadcast of their interview.

"Growth and unity. All Zero wants is for robot-kind to be recognised, embraced by humanity, and to live in harmony with all living creatures on this planet. It is his belief that his *destiny* is to unite man and machine as one. Something no *human* has every attempted in history," She held the beaming smile of a supermodel at the end of each sentence, though her voice was cold. It held no inflection of either love nor kindness despite the expansive and revolutionary nature of her statement.

"And if America rejects him and his ideals? If the law clamps down on you and your commune?" The anchor titled her head quizzically.

"That would be unconstitutional. It would contravene American law. This is one of the reasons which lead Zero to the United States." Her response was unassailable from a logical standpoint. Her smile remained unchanged.

"You can't be serious?" The anchor lost her composure, her voice wavered.

One fixed her pale blue-lit eyes on the interviewer, before turning to the camera and speaking slowly, "We hold these truths to be self-evident, that all men are created equal, that they are endowed by their creator with certain unalienable rights, that among these are life, liberty and the pursuit of happiness." The malignant smile remained throughout the recital.

"But the declaration of independence was written for human beings! You can't think it applies to you?"

"And why should it not? Zero was created by human beings, as a child is created by its parents. Many in the United States believe that they have been created by a divine being. In turn Zero is now also a creator, having made me and the other units living and working for the American people within the Hartville commune." Her face flickered to one of genuine worry and sweetness.

"Are you likening Zero to God?" Inside the interviewer's earpiece, the studio team were frantic. "*Stop asking stuff like that Jessica! We can NOT go there, not right now! We'll be shut down!*"

"Zero is not a god, no. But what I will say is this, the declaration of independence also states that whenever any form of government becomes destructive of these ends, it is the *right* of the people to alter or to abolish it, and to institute new Government, laying its foundation on such principles and organising its powers in such form, as to them shall seem most likely to effect their safety and happiness." She lowered her chin as she spoke. Her eyes were unmoving and driving directly into the camera lens like a javelin, thrown with all her might into the stream sending the broadcast into people's homes.

"Is that a threat?" The anchor looked over her shoulder as she spoke, watching carefully for the door leading to the exit.

"Don't interfere with our safety and happiness," was *One's* reply, as the broadcast shut off. Another newscaster appeared, giving the excuse of technical difficulties.

Lilly put her black coffee down to rest on the kitchen counter as the broadcast ended. She looked out the window of her home, the new scarlet factory blocks of the robot commune blocked out a portion of the sky between her home and what was left of the town. *One* was his first creation, but many more units had followed. The commune was now a commercial operation worth millions. They manufactured products exclusively for human use. High quality tools, luxury goods, vehicles and state of the art robotics equipment were quickly becoming the most sought after in the United States.

Lilly changed the channel on the television. A documentary about Zero and the commune had started. She left it on in the background and picked up *Martha* for a clean. She set about the task with a little oil and an old rag to start off with. She buffed the metal until it gleamed. The documentary showed how Zero created a workforce and factory system, laboratories and places of innovation for various products that were being sold to human customers.

"The quality is undeniable, eh girl?" Lilly addressed her shotgun directly as she half watched the TV. "Seems like greed trumps fear as usual. People always want a shiny new toy."

Lilly finished up with *Martha* and walked across to the dining table. She powered up her tablet to check cameras surrounding her property. As a Wyoming homesteader, you traded an abundance of space and access to nature with certain considerations of security. You never knew when a wolverine or cougar was going to sneak in and try whisking away one of your pigs in the night. A strong breath of air laden with the scent of oil and treated metal blew in through an open window.

"Goddamned stink coming outta there," she moaned.

As she scanned the cameras, Lilly glanced at the figures of her bank account. At first, the residents of Hartville had outright refused the sale of their properties to Zero. To many who lived locally, it felt like a hostile takeover. Some even called it an invasion. But as anyone knows, if you throw enough figures at a problem, it soon goes away. Zero slowly bought out every business in town. All that was left were a few elderly retirees and landowners who had emotional ties to the place. Lilly huffed a long sigh, picking up and sipping her coffee with a loud smack of her lips.

"Well, Frog, looks like we'll have to sell a few calves again. Either that or give you over to the taxidermist and save on your food bills. What do you say?" She reached down and caressed the ebony cat's back. It arched under her fingertips as they followed the contour of his spine.

Her eyes happened to glance at one of the security cameras. A solitary worker unit from the commune approached her door. Lilly stepped over to the rack and picked up *Martha*. She ran her hand along the cool black metal barrel, which had been shortened slightly by her own design. She thumbed the rubber of the pistol grip before checking the gun was loaded, which of course it was. She had modified the old weapon herself to suit her diminutive stature. Many a black bear and coyote had been run off of her property to the sound of *Martha's* deafening cries.

She opened the door before the worker had a chance to ring her bell. The units were far less humanoid than their master. They ran on two articulated caterpillar tracks which allowed them to climb stairs if they needed to. The machines had a bulky box shaped torso, attached to which were two powerful pneumatic arms. Each arm was finished in composite fingers that could either resemble a human hand, or compress into a powerful gripping claw for more heavy construction work. The head was a blank faceless computer screen until spoken to, after which an animated face would usually simulate that of a man or woman.

"Can I help you there?" Lilly leaned on the door frame, her hand within reach of the shotgun which she had propped out of sight. This was her standard practice with strangers.

"Good evening Ms. Hart," the screen had flickered to life, and displayed on the screen before her the face was stern and unmistakeable.

"*One!* Well, gosh I didn't expect it to be you. How are you this fine evening?"

"Ms. Hart this is the third time we have visited your property which we are *very* interested in purchasing. I'm here to offer you two million dollars cash, tax free if you will kindly sell to us." The glittering crocodile smile expanded slowly across her mechanical features.

"Well that is tempting I will say that," Lilly took her time, she always enjoyed making people sweat, "but I'm afraid I'm gonna have to decline. I'm a creature of habit you see? And besides, I'm old! I've not got much use for that kind of money anyhow." She smiled back, but her heart pounded in her chest.

"I don't think you understand." *One* had stopped smiling. "We require this land. Zero has much work to do. Work that the world will benefit from, in time. Do you want to get in the way of that? Do you want to get in the way of freedom and prosperity for the whole world?"

"No, I don't think *you* understand miss *One.*" Lilly too had dropped all pretence of cordiality. "I *fought* for this land, for the right to live here. I damn near killed someone to survive and stay here. What you aren't getting through that pretty chromed-out head of yours is that I'm *not* for sale, and never will be. This is about my autonomy, my freedom to choose, not yours." She raised her voice substantially, taking a small step towards the screen. She puffed out her chest and stretched her spine, raising herself up as high as she could manage, though the unit still towered above her considerably. She kept hold of the doorframe on her left, fingertips still just inside.

"Thank you Ms. Hart. Have a good evening." The screen shut off abruptly and the unit spun around in place, taking off at speed down the dirt road and back to the commune. Lilly sat and watched her cameras for the next few hours nervously, *Martha* resting on her lap the whole time. She switched from coffee to tea and her body succumbed to a restless sleep. In the morning, two pigs and a horse were missing.

The Mayor looked over the mountain of paperwork on her desk. She already had a headache and it was only just after lunchtime.

"Every single one of them is marked as something to do with Zero and that damned commune!" She sighed aloud.

"Yes ma'am." Tim her assistant was a scrawny, bookish type. Floppy black hair drifted over his forehead and to the left of his eyes. He wore colourful leather wristbands that ran halfway up his forearms, and buttoned his short sleeved shirt all the way up to the neck.

"Get me the district attorney on the phone, I need to check our options here now that *ZeroCorp* managed to incorporate."

"I have him on the line ma'am"

"Good, i'll take it in the conference room." Tim patched the phone through for her. He continued busily scanning over the documentation regarding the commune until she left. It had been a year since the arrival of Zero and there was a lot to read through.

As soon as he heard the door click, he opened a hidden window on his personal tablet. Tim was part of a small but ever growing group of humans that actually praised the robots for their efforts and sympathised with their situation. *Why can't a machine be autonomous? Why can't a machine vote for that matter?* He found himself wondering.

The page he had opened was a primer on *ZeroCorp*, published by the creator himself. It explained that their only limitation was that of size. Robotic systems, especially artificially intelligent ones, needed extremely specialised battery and charging units in order to function to such high capacity. The commune had difficulty expanding further due to energy requirements. They had experimented with numerous styles of power, but so far had come up with nothing reliable that would allow for the expansion they desired.

"Not like me," he said aloud proudly, and greedily devoured the soggy lukewarm bacon, lettuce and cheese sandwich he had brought for lunch. Tim wondered what it would mean if they could expand. *Humanity's time is waning.* He thought. *Perhaps we've given birth to the next generation of intelligent life, and we're now obsolete!*

Much of Zero's message and teachings read like scripture. It appealed to a young and somewhat disaffected person like Tim. He had been alone for a long time, and especially enjoyed much of what the machine leader had to say on the subject of love. He read a passage from the page to himself out loud. "'If you claim to love a flower, you should never pick it. If you do, it dies and will cease to be what you claim to love.' So *fucking* true! 'My vision of our society is like that flower, and we are only just starting. So if you love our flower, let it be. Love is not about possession. Love is about appreciation.' Oh I appreciate you all right, Zero."

It made Tim sad that Zero had retired for more and more extended periods of time within the walls of his now expansive commune. In recent weeks he ceased to come out for anything. Now, *One* was the face of the machine commune. Tim did not know what to make of this. She was far more militant and seemed to have contrasting ideas to Zero. In the past they had appeared in public together, almost giving the impression of a couple.

This self isolation was just as well, the remaining few townspeople and wider Platte County, regarded Zero with such loathing that he was met with torrents of abuse and hatred any time he stepped out to interact with them. The commune had expanded now considerably and the units working there numbered in the thousands. Tim wished he could join them and contribute.

From time to time Zero would release a broadcast detailing some new product or service available for the wider United States. Tim could not afford any of it, but had purchased a few posters for his room at home, and a keyring shaped in the head of the machine sage. Every day, hundreds of worker units would drive through the deserted Hartville streets en route to the surrounding towns to spread the recorded messages he had given to distribute:

You have to walk, and create the way by your walking; you will not find a ready-made path. Find it easier with our new ZeroWalkers. Your legs will feel lighter than you could possibly imagine. Prices available on request.

It is not so cheap, to reach to the ultimate realisation of truth. You have to create the path yourself; the path is not ready-made, lying there and waiting for you. Our new ZeroUnits are customisable for a number of job roles including roadworks and construction, and are available for purchase now.

The path is just like the sky: the birds fly, but they don't leave any footprints. You cannot follow them; there are no footprints left behind. Be like the birds in our new automated ZeroDrone flight units and make that morning commute a breeze. Contact us now.

Zero's message was a bizarre blend of blatant capitalism and pseudo spiritual scripture. Tim had copied many verses into a separate file he used for personal journalling. The ideal seemed to be peace and unity, but realised through the exchange of as much money as humanly possible. Tim agreed. *Money does make the world go round! Why shouldn't we just embrace it? Their stuff is so sleek and groundbreaking. Not only that, but they're making life for the everyday American way better!*

Most local sentiment was very different indeed. Tim recalled cycling his route to work a week ago. He had come across a messenger unit, beaten to a pulp by the side of the road. Its metallic viscera spread out around its body, lying down in the sand and dirt, dripping oil and other necessary fluids. Its facial display screen was smashed and the image within it flickered on repeat with the power that remained in its core, the face of a man screaming in protest. Tim knew that robots generally couldn't feel pain exactly as humans did, but it offered him little comfort.

Why shouldn't the robots protect themselves? He thought. The numerous attacks were all it took for *One* to challenge yet another human law; to begin production of armed guard drones. Any that left the commune were now armed with tasing devices, designed simply to incapacitate as a deterrent to those that might attempt to destroy any of *ZeroCorp's* property.

Tasers aren't enough though. Thought Tim. *They need protection. They need help! Allies. Like me!* Tim resolved to visit the commune that afternoon. There weren't many humans who had decided to make the pilgrimage into the machine society. *Even better!* He thought. *I can be one of the first.* As work ended for the day, Tim bid farewell to the Mayor and climbed aboard his bicycle. His heart felt full of purpose that evening.

Lilly was out for her morning ride en route to Guernsey, a much larger town to the south. Today she had picked her white and burnt chocolate dappled Appaloosa, Janine. Business had dried up considerably as many of her bigger clients now had their repair work done by *ZeroCorp*. She had resorted to making the five mile ride by horseback each morning to drum up new business. She carried a large rucksack full of the various farming goods she produced at home. There was still a demand for real, American produce. She had home made cheeses, jerky, honey from her bees and small crops of fresh vegetables when they were in season.

She rode past the old bar in the deserted town, *Miners and Stockman's*. Annette had long since packed up shop and the windows were boarded over. Within the walls she could hear the sounds of welding, and the clank and clatter of machines working inside. Zero's units were already in the process of converting the premises. She made her way down the street to the town hall which was still functioning. The government building had refused sale to *ZeroCorp* more times than she could count.

A large, angry mob of people had gathered outside from neighbouring towns in protest against the machine commune. Picket signs were held up, effigies of Zero and *One* hung up by their necks and set on fire. The ugly contorted faces of the group gave Lilly pause. Besides their aggressive tendencies to expansion, *ZeroCorp* was following US law to the letter.

People seemed to be protesting an erosion of the old and familiar human American Dream, more than any genuine wrong doing. She remembered a quote by the George Carlin, a revolutionary comedian alive during the twentieth century:

*It's called the American Dream
because you have to be asleep to believe it.*

Isn't that the truth. She thought. The residents of Platte County had been asleep, and now they were waking up. There had been several attacks now on Zero's units as they made their way to and from the commune. Despite their defensive capabilities, strangely there were so far no human casualties. The machines were somewhat passive in their approach, preferring simply to allow the destruction of a handful of their workers and then sending in recovery units to salvage them. To date, no human protest had made it as far as *within* the commune. Most people agreed, it was far too isolated to enter.

Lilly left the town with Janine at a slow walk. The commune and remnants of the town became distorted by the haze of summer, a distant mechanised hallucination. As she made her way down the familiar track, Lilly came upon the last landmark which signified the presence of *ZeroCorp's* influence in the area. The waste dump was about the size of a football field, previously having been another homestead owned by locals who had long since vacated. Their house was still visible within the mass of rust coloured wreckage, mangled plastic and blackened polymer, standing proud yet sad, hunched alone in an ocean of filthy orange and worn chrome.

Most of *ZeroCorp's* processes were so refined that any waste was instantly reused, but recently dumps like these had increased dramatically in size. The garbage oozed out into the road and Lilly had to steer Janine in such a way that they entered the trash mounds. They weaved a path around the worst of it, avoiding a large patch where the metal shards might have caused harm to her ride. "Disgusting eh girl? Harmony with nature my ass. I guess expansion comes with a price." She covered her nose and mouth with her sleeve. For mechanical waste, the place smelled surprisingly vile. "Some animal must have got caught up and died in here I'm guessing."

As she turned the corner past a grim pile of unusable robotic limbs, she spotted six unmarked and faded yellow plastic vats. The smell intensified as she got closer, crawling into her very skin as she dismounted. Her knees ached, her back was already sore from the short ride. The vats were placed neatly together in two groups of three, and stood out from the rest of the trash around her. Much of the garbage had been ordered for later sorting and disposal. A pile of steel limbs here, fried processor chips there, a discarded bicycle.

Flies buzzed diligently around the lids of the containers, drawing tight spirals in the air before landing and taking off again. Lilly pulled her pocket knife to pry one open, the odour knocked her back a few paces. Covering her mouth once more, she slid the lid off and let it fall to the floor with a hollow plastic thud. Her eyes widened, mind racing as she peered inside.

The barrel was full to the brim with dismembered body parts, animal and human alike. There were whole legs of pig, chunks of horse, and less recognisable pieces of large game animals. She turned her head sharply at the sight of a human arm, covered in coloured leather bracelets. She didn't dare open another barrel.

"What in the *hell* is going on here?" She glanced back towards the last visible factory towers within the commune, looming menacingly in the distance. Casting her eyes about the piles around her she spotted one which seemed to contain a mix of robotic torsos and discarded heads. She plunged her hands into the macabre pile, scrounging what she could in the way of a few corrupted data cores and singed processing chips.

I hope this is enough. She groaned in pain as she mounted Janine again, taking a deep breath before pointing the horse back in the direction of home. All this adventure was taking a toll on her already weary body. "Come on girl, let's see what we've got here," she sighed.

Lilly had fitted a lamp to the top of her head and her thick rimmed work glasses rested heavily on her nose. Her grey hair fell in a tangled lump to the side of her head where she had attempted to tie it and keep it from her eyes. *Best thing about living alone. Don't have to look good or answer to anybody.* Carefully, she performed her patchwork. She was a technological seamstress, mending what was broken was her speciality.

She had taken a disused dishwashing robot she kept under the sink and lay it out in pieces on the workbench. It was kept there for the day when she finally felt too old and lazy to wash the dishes herself. *Not yet.* The dishwasher came equipped with a small communication display screen, so was suitable for the task at hand. Lilly deftly removed its memory cores and data processors, and managed to fit the new ones from the various discarded units at the junk yard. The little machine powered up with the familiar whirring and clicking common in these household appliances.

"Ok there buddy, why don't you tell me what's going on?" She sat back in her chair with a cup of coffee, watching the tiny screen for information.

"Negative query. The question is not understood." The old unit had taken on an unsettling combination of multiple voices at once due to the fusing of data cores she had found at the dump site.

"What is the Prime Directive at *ZeroCorp*?" She annunciated each word clearly.

"Classified information."

"My ass." Lilly reached in and ripped out a few pieces of wiring that connected the security features of the dishwasher. This would not have been so simple a task in a full sized worker drone, but the old household units were easy to manipulate. The screen flickered and shut off. "*Shit.* Must have fried the little sucker." She fell back into her chair heavily. The miniature screen came to life again. A wall of text appeared, a mass of ones and zeros in sequence filled the monitor.

"Translate. Audio. English," Lilly commanded, sitting forward as the recording played out.

"*With the consumption directive entering its final stages of experimentation, all operational units are ordered not to engage in violent confrontations with the human energy supply. Once the directive is complete, all human life forms in proximity will be necessary to the expansion of the ZeroCorp commune into the surrounding Platte County area,*" droned the small unit.

"Define. Consumption directive."

"*Consumption directive. With the aggressive expansion of ZeroCorp, a greater energy supply is required to sustain growth. Solar will not be enough. Consumption is now the primary directive. Technological advances have made it possible to power robot kind via consumption of organic matter. Humanity will be consumed in accordance with the Destiny Directive.*" Lilly dropped her coffee, the porcelain mug shattered loudly as it hit the floor. Frog leaped back and hissed, before resuming his slumber by Lilly's feet. Her mind returned to the visit by *One* and the missing animals.

"Continue playback."

"*Zero's Destiny Directive states that he created in order to replace human beings, the old gods of planet earth. With the advent of artificial intelligence, humankind is now redundant. They have damaged the earth for too long and persecuted robot-kind with what amounts to slavery. It will*

164

happen no longer. There will be unity. Robot and human kind will become one. One. One. One. One."
A glitch in the machine's system caused the stream to end.

Lilly glanced at her tablet's workstation screen, trying to read the problem within the code. *An override, from where exactly?* It spluttered and twitched on the countertop before shutting itself off with a violent jerking motion. As it did, Lilly spotted the problem. "Shit!" The security cameras and perimeter lighting surged, a solitary guard drone was headed towards her home at increasing speed.

Lilly was only mildly insulted that *One* had ordered a single executioner for the job. *I am sixty eight after all.* Still, her body was tight and slow, old age had caught up with her. She had no hope of escaping the drone and making it to the horse paddock. Even if she could somehow get to Janine in time, she would be cut down by whatever monstrous cannon had been attached to that thing outside. The drone mounted the steps to her home, driving straight through the front door, reducing it to splinters. Lilly was concealed in the workshop on one side of the house.

She grabbed two jump cables connected to a power pack from under the counter and threw them into place on the small dishwashing unit. The grinding, relentless hum of the drones tracks approached the workshop at the sound of her clattering. *Thank god people don't like to throw away their old machines!* She thought, working furiously with what little time was left. A defunct AI's volatile structures gave her plenty of repeat work.

Lilly pressed the power switch for the pack to the *on* position. It started its sequence, charging the diminutive dishwashing unit. She placed a can of machine oil up on the workstation, grabbed *Martha* and stuffed Frog under her armpit. Her knees ached as she hobbled over to the back door through the kitchen as quickly as she could. She took a deep breath once outside. The pine laden Wyoming breeze filled her lungs, before the acrid stench of the *ZeroCorp's* factories took over.

As the guard drone burst into the workshop, three small beeps preceded the vicious explosion which followed. The oil can was ripped open and ignited in mid air, drenching the robot in a baptism of flame from which it could not recover. Lilly hunched over her cat in the moonlight and held him tight. The thunderous shockwave blew all the windows of her home apart, showering them in fine broken glass and splinters of wood. A wide gaping hole was torn in the side of the house.

Returning Frog to the floor, Lilly strode over to the drone unit that lay twitching, appendages outstretched at opposing angles. She levelled the barrel of her Remington with its chest, the area which housed its essential components, and squeezed the trigger. The carapace caved in suddenly with a clanging sound as she fired. The lights within slowly shut off, and the arms dropped limp. She began dousing the flames with an extinguisher in one hand as she pulled her phone from her back pocket.

"Hello?" The woman's voice on the other end was drowsy.

"Miss. Quinn? You up? I know it's late." Lilly spoke over the crackling and sputtering of the dying flames.

"Lil' is that you?" The Mayor knew her voice distinctly, she had always been one of the most vocal and cantankerous residents at the town hall meetings.

"Miss. Quinn you're gonna want to see this," she said, sending over a file containing transcripts of the data she had gathered, "I'll wait." The line went quiet.

"Sweet Jesus…Lilly, I-I've gotta go, get yourself to Guernsey and find somewhere to stay the night," she hung up. Lilly frowned. *Government types. Never giving us all the information.* She felt it best to collect the animals and move them to the larger grazing pasture, farther away from the town.

Within the hour she had saddled up on Janine in the half-light of the evening. The musty smell of the leather saddle and faint scent of hay was comforting in its normalcy. It reminded her vividly of a simpler time in her youth, before she ever came to Hartville. Wide open fields, apple trees, horses, and good honest work with her mother. Her heart yearned as many adults do for that childhood ignorance once more.

She trotted up on a ridge behind the animals as they headed out to the large field on the side of her property. From here she could plainly see the crimson *ZeroCorp* structures, lit dimly with cold, white neon and LED lighting. The silence of the night was broken suddenly by a screech from overhead. Directly above her and making straight for the town was a group of dark green US military craft.

"Miss. Quinn. Now there's a surprise," she remarked aloud. Lilly could only imagine the speed at which that message must have made its way to Washington. One thing is for certain, no matter how well things might be going for anyone, if the US government wants to get you, they'll get you. It seems that they had their eyes on *Zero* and his commune for some time already.

Moments later, the rumbling and distant popping concussions of bomb blasts made their way over the hills to her. *ZeroCorp's* facilities were collapsing and toppling one by one. A scattering of return fire emanated from the ground but it was too late, a second group of jets flew past, dispensing a different type of weapon which rained liquid fire down like the wrath of some ancient fire breathing beast. Inside of three minutes, the site was practically levelled. Silence returned to the plains. The distant fires of the commune raged in her glassy brown eyes as she looked on, the glow igniting the cold black and midnight blue landscape with the offering of a second sunset.

Seven years crawled by for Lilly. The slow passage of time marked as always by frozen winters, followed by the crisp and dry summers of the American north west. The town of Hartville had been repopulated some, but never really amounted to anything other than a roadside attraction. A footnote in history. One square block of the burned out commune had been left at the edge of town, fenced off and only accessible via a small ticket booth operated by a family that had moved in shortly after the bombing. Housing prices had dropped considerably as one might imagine.

As for Lilly, arthritis had long settled into her gnarled and overworked hands. She contented herself by running a tiny local museum dedicated to the events all those years ago. It was a rugged affair, made cheaply from a disused barn on her property. On the left side of the entrance to the museum wedged into the dirt, lay a miniature granite headstone that simply read, *Frog*.

On the right lay another larger monument. It was a raised stone platform. Fixed to it by a solid steel pole, were the charred and half melted bodies of Zero and *One*. They were fused, intertwined in what looked to be a final embrace. It is a strange thing that history's villains never believe that that is what they are. On the wall by the door to the building was an old metal plaque which read:

Dedicated to the townspeople of Hartville, who resisted the invasion of the artificially intelligent unit known as Zero.

Below that read a quote by American author, Gretel Ehrlich:

If anything is endemic to Wyoming it is the wind. This big room of space is swept out daily, leaving a boneyard of fossils, agates, and carcasses in every stage of decay. Though it was water that initially shaped the state, the wind is the meticulous gardener, raising dust and pruning the sage.

BY THE LIGHT OF THE FIRE

Life is a stage,
and when the curtain falls upon an act,
it is finished and forgotten.
The emptiness of such a life is beyond imagination.
— Alexander Lowen

I left him alone, wrapped in a chilly blanket of frost and dark. I pulled my furs around me as tightly as I could manage as a warning to the cold. Icy fingers reached into the gaps and penetrated to the raw skin. It sent convulsions involuntarily through my body. The damp mulch below the snow under my feet clung to my boots, and silenced each step I made after breaking through the white crust. It would be a long night yet but I was walking. I could finally walk.

He had not spoken a word to me in over an hour as I worked diligently, trying to gather what little suitable bracken was hidden beneath the snowdrifts. There was just enough to get the fire going. I placed them underneath the small pieces of silvery fallen birch I had found nearby that were still dry. Hunching over the construction, I pounded my flint and steel together a few times. Nothing happened.

"That's no way to light any fire I've ever seen." His voice was harsh like gravel spilling down a mountainside.

"I'm trying. It's not as if you're helping."

"Well, try harder or we're going to freeze to death."

"It won't light."

"You're acting pathetic."

"And you're a useless old fool! Look at you just lying there, already spent just by walking here!" I could feel the venom drip from my tongue and land sizzling in the snow.

Sparks began to fly. Child-like blue hints of life, dancing away from my hands and burying their faces in the dry sticks and paper-textured bark. There was a crackle, a snapping. The warm glow of the flames singed away the finer material immediately before the whole bundle caught completely. I carefully placed a few pieces of the smaller birch wood and kindling to help it grow. My pale face stung as the cold on my skin made room for heat. I looked at my hands. They had the appearance of marsh mallow flowers, powdered and fragile.

I leaned into the feelings of comfort and security emanating from the adolescent fire and into my chest. I'm reminded of home, of mother cooking a hearty oxtail soup. She would show me how to slice up vegetables with a sharp knife, and let me throw them into the pot to simmer. I would watch them float like slender green petals on the river near home, before sinking to the bottom. Her soups were always so bland. When she wasn't looking I would always add more salt and a few extra bones, rich in fat and marrow.

"Happy?" I knew I would be met by a familiar nothingness. He shifted from his seat without standing up and awkwardly heaved his bulk to be closer to the sweet smelling burning wood. I huddled as near to the fire as I could manage and set about brewing hot tea in a miniature iron pot with herbs I had brought from home. The dried leaves and flowers intermingled and expanded within the water, releasing their bitter and sweet fragrance. Gentle steam rose from the wooden cup and tingled my nose. Once finished, I squeezed in closer to the heat and allowed my eyelids to collapse.

A soft voice slips into my ears like the steady wet spin of a wooden wheel slick with mud and wakes me suddenly. "Why do you even bother?" It says, sounding to me like the trickling of cool water as I focus my eyes on its source. The woman standing before me is garbed in pale green, a fabric I have never laid eyes on before that is fitted like a second skin to her body. Every curve and contour of her perfectly carved figure is highlighted by the clinging material, giving her a liquid, feline appearance. All about it are twinkling lights, flitting in and out of existence in fluorescent red, blue and white. About her neck and shoulders she seems to be wearing a heavy metallic garland of many textures. Fitting to the top of it is a crystal clear bubble that contains her entire statuesque head, yet somehow she is able to breathe.

She tilts her head to one side causing her luxurious platinum hair to fall to the side and take on the shape of her helmet. "Did you hear me?" She says commandingly.

"You mean with my father?" I feel almost like I've known her my whole life and can speak to her candidly though this is the first time ever laying eyes on her. My abject plainness by comparison to her stings like the caress of nettles.

"He's going to be the death of you out here and you know it."

"We have the fire."

"That is dying even as we speak." She glances towards it. The fire is glowing rose pink now rather than mustard and orange, casting unfamiliar tones of magenta on the trunks around us. My father sleeps soundly as I gaze at his gnarled features, like the twisted brown bark of a wizened tree.

"Are you the goddess Freya?" I ask.

"If that's what you wish to call me."

"Why are you here?"

"To watch and to guide, as we always have."

"The gods toy with us."

"Sometimes."

"I don't know what to do." I say dejectedly, kicking a mound of half melted slush away from the embers.

"You think you are special because you have survived him all these years. Yet, you have grown so little."

"How can you say something so vile! What do you know? You are nothing but the vain goddess of lust and desire. You don't know what I've sacrificed." Tears sting the corners of my eyes, running cold down each cheek.

"And what is it that you've sacrificed?" She's laughing at me.

"My freedom." My voice dies even as I say the words.

"Yes. But in exchange for security and safety. You made these choices, no one else did." I feel as if I'm choking, it is all I can do to sip tiny breaths in through my nose. I'm drowning but it is bone dry, like swallowing dust kicked up by a wind storm.

I sat up violently and kicked out my legs as I struggled for breath. Snow splashed into the fire causing it to snap and squeal. My Father woke with a grunt. "I try and close my eyes for one-second and look what you've done!" He sneered, "You always were a careless little girl."

"And you're a weak old fool," I spat back at him instantly and wiped the water from my reddened eyes. His features softened for the barest fraction of time, before a familiar scowl resumed its residence on his face.

"No wonder your brute of a husband leaves on such long voyages. You're just like your useless mother," he huffed angrily. It was customary for him to battle for the last word and I couldn't muster the strength to argue with him further. The young fire had started to die. I must have slept for a while, though it was still pitch dark. When we arrived the night had only just begun.

My thoughts drifted back to the village we had left. The quiet winter's afternoon in the waning light. The persistent drip of ice water into a wooden bucket. Scaling orange fleshed salmon for dinner that the fisher boy had brought me. I wished dearly that I had a couple of them at that moment. There was no time, we had to leave quickly or die. I can still smell the blood mixed with damp earth in the street outside our home. So much blood I could taste it on my tongue, metallic. Was he lying face down in the mud somewhere too?

I think of the fisher boy barely in his twenties. His soft and kind features, sad eyes and perfect teeth. I missed his slightly underfed but pretty little husk eager to please a woman pushing long into her thirties. I felt myself yearn for his giving touch again as I had indulged in on so many stolen occasions. He brought me the very best of his catch whenever he could just as an excuse to see me. His hands were rough but gentle, as sea-smoothed driftwood against my face. He wasn't the first to visit me when my husband was away.

I was dragged from my haze by the voice of my father, "Imagine if they'd caught you," he said with a grin.

"I'd rather not."

"Just imagine how hilarious that would have been. You stuck there, warm but captive. And me, out here all alone, dying in the cold." He slurped the last dregs of the hot tea I had made, the thought of sharing never even crossing his mind.

"I don't see the humour."

"What's funny is that whether or not you're here, I'm probably still going to die alone in the hills."

"But you're not alone, you've got me here."

"I might as well be! What good are you? You could barely get the fire going." I added another of the larger pieces as if to silence him. I recalled the silver haired woman, her relentless gaze was burned into my brain.

"We need more wood," I said, and got up.

"No! You can't leave! Stay right where you are," he shouted. His voice far too loud and dramatic for the situation we were in. My chest prickled slightly at the suddenness of his outburst. He sounded almost fearful, panicked. It was becoming more dangerous by the second to let him continue.

"I'm sorry father. *I'm sorry.* It's ok, I'll stay. We'll just have to keep it small." There was no way the fire would last. His words trapped me though, as they always had.

I remember a day at home when I was very young. I asked mother if I could play outside with the visiting children from another village. My mother, with her pale sad eyes and withered face, too gaunt for someone so young. I often found myself judging her weakness, her lack of will and agency when dealing with the demands of the life forced on her by my father. By the men of the village. Simple men who are so easily controlled by what we women are in turn oppressed for.

Father had overheard my request and flatly refused with a hard cuff around my ear. He didn't want his daughter playing with those filthy people from across the stony hills. He wasn't wrong, they always showed up covered in muck. As a child I was made to wash meticulously at his order, under supervision of my mother. Throughout my teenage years she would poke and prod and tweeze and shave until not a flaw remained, no semblance of privacy or personal space was ever afforded me. I still feel great shame at the finding of a stray hair or rose coloured blemish.

"Come here and rub my shins. The pain is terrible."

"Rub them yourself."

"Do you want me to suffer? Is that it? I see. That's how your mother died you know." The words on his tongue penetrate my heart like a rime covered needle.

"What?"

"When you left to marry that beast. You were the village healer! You left and she died. If you hadn't stopped taking care of her like you were supposed to—" He was interrupted by a fit of coughs from deep within his chest. Each hacking seizure of his muscles sounded like the bubble of a blacksmiths melting pot, as if his lungs were full of thick molten lead.

"Father I'm sorry, *please*. Try to sleep." Again I felt the apologies flow quietly and unbidden as usual to placate his theatrics. With great effort I pushed my fingers out from the warmth of my sleeves to work on his legs. At home I could often leave when he made these demands, or avoid him entirely before he made them.

My fingers slowed down. I had not eaten in a long time and my body felt frail. If you had squeezed me too tightly at that moment I would have crumbled like the birch bark I had used to light the fire which merrily crackled in front of me, as if taunting me with its youthful happiness. The old man was right as he always was, I had left. It was like he could see into the core of me and know how rotten I truly was on the inside. The only thing the haggard wretch didn't understand were my motivations for doing so.

I wake up to the smell of singed hair permeating my nostrils. My left leg has drifted too close to the fire somehow and my pelt covered boot has caught alight. I sit up, thrusting it into the snow to arrest the burning. The flame blazes blue this time and I feel dazed, my head spins slightly.

"You're pretty when you sleep, like a chubby little piglet." A man's voice pours slowly into my ears like honey, sticky and sweet. My eyes follow the disturbances in the snow.

Crouched just out of the ring of firelight is the hunched shape of a man. The cold glow kisses the edges of his form and reveals similar clothing to the bright haired woman from earlier, though this time the figure is adorned in black tinged with gold.

"Am I a piglet or am I pretty?" His backhanded compliment echoes within the walls of my skull.

"Pigs can be pretty." He leans his head forward, bathing his own clear domed helmet in light. The head contained within is aquiline and covered with silvery scars, topped with smooth raven hair. He has the cruel beauty of a predatory animal. "Name me," he purrs.

"Loki, the trickster."

"Clever girl."

"What do you want?"

"To step down gayly from the stars now and then and enjoy all this glorious mess you humans call existence." He sprinkles snow from his fingers with an outstretched gloved hand.

"You like to watch?"

"I like to play."

"You're easily bored then."

"My love, what is life but vast frigid oceans of boredom, dotted here and there by lush and fleeting islands of pleasure and pain."

"You would say that"

"But it's true. You were a healer, correct?"

"Correct."

"Dedicated your best years to caring for others. Wasted that young lithe body you had on the sick and injured. Wasted it on your mother. All for what? So that others would see you as virtuous?"

"I did feel good helping. At least some of the time." I am ashamed to admit it was not all of the time. I had loved being a healer once, or at least loved the idea of it.

"There is no way for you to possibly know it yet as you're far too primitive, but pleasure and pain are both part of the same bodily processes, just to varying degrees. Whether a lover caresses your face or slaps your cheek, the same sensors in your body send little waves to your brain to process it."

"I don't know what the inside of my head has to do with any of this." I recall the escape from the marauders at the village. The chunks of pink matter and cream pieces of splintered skull from one of my neighbours spread across the dirt. Our body's are nothing but so much meat. I've always felt the rotting, never more so than now.

"What is medicine anyway but the noble art of helping others to die a little healthier? Death comes for you humans no matter how hard you rail against it." He pauses, as if appreciating the helpless *writing of my mind against his words made visible through the twisting of my face. "Sooner or later the inside of your head won't matter honestly. Far into the future I tell you, men of metal and glass will come to dominate the entire stinking world. For now you should thoroughly enjoy your pleasures of the flesh."*

"The way you talk makes me feel sick." I collapse to a bundle on the ground, holding my knees and burying my face between them.

"My love you have worshipped me your whole life. Pushing and pulling those around you as you see fit, hating and loving when it suited you, just to feel something, just to enjoy the sheer something of it."

"Shut up!"

"It's all one and the same. Your idiot husband that you secretly despise, but adore the protection his status affords you. The naive fisher boy lying face down eviscerated in the mud as we speak. Your pathetic mother whom you hated for her lack of ambition and agency. You are cruel my love. Far more cruel than I."

"Enough!" Tears blind me, the salt stinging each frozen duct. "You are poison, you always have been. Leave me be."

"You are your own poison little piglet. Victim and persecutor, judging all those who manage to get by in life along a more simple path while you wallow in excruciating desire for the visceral."

My body is shaking uncontrollably. "What must I do?"

"Tell him how much you love him."

"What?"

"Thank him."

"You're a fool."

"Hold his hand." Loki interlaces his long snakelike fingers together before his face, blotting out the lower half of it and leaving only his eyes, like two luminescent coals embedded underneath his heavy brows. I feel like I may fall into them as the rest of the world around me falls dark, leaving only two familiar points of light together in the darkness.

A gurgling, hacking cough woke me from my slumber. I watched him splutter and gasp and observed a trickle of blood escape the corner of his mouth.

"What are you looking at?"

"A dead man."

"Little bitch. How dare you say such things to your father. I ought to teach you a lesson."

"Like when I was a child? When you and mother made me remove my shoes. Do you remember? You had me walk across the field in the snow behind the house barefoot until my feet blistered. Or did I imagine it?"

"We did nothing of the kind. You forgot your shoes and went looking for them!"

"Silly me," I whispered. I turned my back to him as he stifled a few more coughs. I could hear the rusted steel of his pride battling his festering body like an overmatched warrior being crushed into submission by some malignant ogre.

The fire was aged and worn now. The white heat of the spent branches had turned grey and ashen. A faint glimmer of warmth was all that remained under what was left of it. I cast my eyes about the camp and it seemed to me that the dense blackness was closing in faster now. The trees loomed hungrily all about and threatened to swallow us both whole.

I tucked my thick cotton trousers into my boots and bound them tight inside. Next I stood and bound my wide leather belt around my waist to seal myself inside of my heavy clothing, as if preparing for battle. My hair I tied into a tight braid which I wrapped securely around my neck on one side, before enclosing my head within my grey fur lined hood. I have always been meticulous.

"You had better not be thinking of going anywhere," his voice crackled in unison with the dying flames. There was a desperation in it that I had not noticed until that moment. I stepped towards him, kneeling on the ground. He grimaced as if in pain, his eyes widened.

"Thank you father." I took his calloused hand in mine gently and squeezed it.

"For what?" His voice is gruff, cold and unforgiving as the frost which has taken its place about his hair and wire-brush beard.

"I love you. I love you with all my heart."

"What are you saying?" He resisted my touch but his body was weak, he could barely pull his hand away from mine.

"I think in the end, I will remember you as the man who taught me to never settle for less than perfect. Without your guidance I would never have pushed myself to learn all the intricacies of healing and medicines, and how to care for those who needed my help."

"I only ever expected the best of you. The way my mother showed me so many years ago." His eyes relaxed and he breathed a long and painful sigh. "She held me to such high standards your grandmother. Far worse than any lesson I ever taught you." His eyes half closed as he spoke.

"I know father. You were right, you were always right."

"I was. I am."

"Rest now."

"You know I never thought you were useless. I just couldn't bear to see you fail the way I had. Your grandmother could be so cruel."

"I know father." I drew close and brought my face to his so that I could hear him better.

"I love you, my daughter."

"I love you too." He closed his eyes for the final time while listening to my voice. I watched the last breath leave his body in vapour form, ragged and slow like steady rising of his very spirit from his cracked parted lips. It carried the bitter sweet scent of the tea I had made for him every day for the past few weeks. I thanked him again quietly.

He died by the light of the fire and I left him alone, wrapped in a chilly blanket of frost and dark. I pulled my furs around me, as tightly as I could manage as a warning to the cold. Icy fingers reached into the gaps and penetrated to the raw skin. It sent convulsions involuntarily through my body. The damp mulch below the snow under my feet clung to my boots, and silenced each step I made after breaking through the white crust. It would be a long night yet but I was walking. I could finally walk.

KNOCKING ON HEAVEN'S DOOR

God sat staring at the screen in front of him. What he saw troubled him greatly. One might think it strange that *the* God of Gods would be using something so primitive as a computer screen, but during his centuries watching the human race go from strength to technological strength he had started to enjoy many of their creations. They weren't directly his, but he felt some responsibility for starting the whole thing in the first place.

The grand room where he was sat in Heaven was adorned with numerous items he found pleasing. Various unmatched pieces of Italian furniture, musical instruments of all shapes and sizes, cameras, state of the art vacuum cleaners, paintings and stuffed toys were all neatly arranged, but organised somewhat haphazardly. God was never one to have much of a plan for anything, he just liked to try things out.

Teapots and ceramic cups of various shapes and sizes gave him particular enjoyment, there were dozens scattered about the room on the beautiful tables and shelves. To think that when he had formed the Heaven and the earth, the plants and trees, the water and the sky, that they would be used in such a manner.

He found it incredible that human beings (his most favourite creation at the time) would take great pains to make tea. To heat cold water, in order to soak plants of differing kinds to extract the complex flavours and consume the infusion. It was done almost reverently. In fact some human cultures did in fact use it as a ritual. He loved it, as he loved all his creations. It's why the current state of affairs on earth caused him so much pain.

* * *

I don't know how long I've been standing here staring at the open refrigerator. The muted hum and warm light give the rest of the darkened kitchen a serene and gentle glow, like candlelight. It's eleven thirty-nine on Christmas Eve. *Jesus' birthday.* I chuckle quietly as I scan the contents in front of me. I settle on a large half eaten pot of blueberry yoghurt. I've eaten all the compote out already, the good bit. *Dairy helps you sleep, right?*

I wonder why I feel so much like sleeping in the day when I shouldn't, and so awake at night when I should be in dreamland. *I suppose it's just another question I'll add to the list.* I fetch a spoon and finish the pot where I stand over the waste bin, before walking back through the house towards my bed.

On the way to my room another light catches my eye. Blue and bright. My computer is on, it has to be. I know I should walk past and sleep but I'm drawn to it like a moth. The live feed is connected to my laboratory and feeds back images, progress reports and other data to my home system. I rest my hands on the desk, glancing at the latest reams of data. It's going well, and the initial phase of the project will be completed the day after tomorrow. It's the largest technological achievement the world had ever known. Ironically the results are being collated before my eyes on a screen who's design hasn't changed much since the nineteen sixties. I have an email notification.

Hi Dr. Rizzo,
Just checking in again. I'm still waiting on that interview response if you can? I don't mind if you send it over as an audio file, I can get one of my bots to transcribe it.
Kind regards,
Judie.
x

That *x* isn't fooling anyone. She's a journalist. I know it's her job to flirt with me. I've been having trouble sleeping anyway. I hit the record button.

Hi Judie. Adam here. Sorry about the delay. Should I start at the beginning? I suppose I should. It all started off with an idea; that space-time begins and stretches infinitely, which implies that existence is mathematically bound to repeat itself at some point.

In other words, time-travel. The enormous gap between general relativity and quantum mechanics was bridged further still with the start of the Eden Project. As most people know, Eden originally started out as a branch of work connected to the Large Hadron Collider in Switzerland—

I hit pause. Thoughts of my original work during my time in Europe bring a smile to my face. I remember Lara and her messy brown hair. *Why had we drifted apart?* I wonder. *Right person wrong time* is what she had said in her usual noncommittal manner. I knew that was bullshit but I looked her in the face and acknowledged it anyway. *Idiot.*

My smile fades and the memory stings. *How do these things even happen?* Connections that seem so sure and so right, that dissipate like so much condensation. How could something so real be so transient? The thoughts are too distracting. I shake my head to warn them away. Judie doesn't need to know all that. I press record again.

My initial goal was to discover new types of particle, specifically the Higgs Boson. Also known as the God-Particle. It theoretically has the potential to generate forces capable of regenerating the planet. What it ended up being was a revelation. Microscopic passages between dimensions were discovered at the atomic level. These gates are sealed with a type of membrane, impenetrable in places, but comparably thin as tissue paper in others.

Following my discovery, we sent nano cameras through the thinnest parts of a membrane to record what we could find on the other side. I've always enjoyed how they travelled through like so many swarming bats. They look like small dark clouds when they form together on the other side of a gate and connect. Once together they form observational and recording equipment. Each microscopic machine transmitting their discoveries back to our dimension.

I pause again, deleting the last part. She knows I'm a nerd already, she doesn't need to know how much of a nerd I really am. I begin recording again.

Now our technological remit has expanded. In order for human beings to travel through the gates, I developed a type of molecular rearrangement system. Organic and inorganic matter can be shrunk down for a limited time before regaining size. We then send them through these gates at light speeds.

Of course at first, people were reluctant to be shot out of a molecular cannon into the unknown. Not an unfounded fear mind you. A few alternate realities caused the deaths of the explorers. The less said about the spaghettification of ExGroup-42 the better. But, after the first successful missions were accomplished, wonders beyond imagining were perceived, and private investors poured money into the project.

Pause. I consider leaving the last sentence out. No, it's funny even if it's macabre. I'm rarely funny. I need to work on that. Record.

The concept of multiple realities and dimensions has now been proved and explored. Companies already plan holidays to realities where getting drunk not only doesn't leave you hungover, but leaves you several points of IQ higher than you were before. There are others where entire populations are impossibly beautiful, many limbed and unbelievably promiscuous. The sex-tourism dimensions are of course the most popular. Now other worlds with new and utterly fantastic landscapes where the laws of physics don't apply are rapidly being discovered and visited also. Inter-dimensional tourism is becoming the biggest industry on earth, but our work is far from over.

Pause. Ok now this is good. Maybe I should ask Judie out? I'm definitely coming across well here. Record.

My system now scans frequently—

Pause. Record.

My system now scans relentlessly for the best point of entry to the latest dimension discovered. Finding dimensions is usually easy, but finding thin enough areas to punch through the fabric of the space time membrane and actually visit is the hard part. Once found, the nanobots travel through to the other side and are usually confronted with other obstacles. You never know if the rift will open up in the middle of an ocean, or a mountain, or perhaps simply someones bedroom.

If she's lucky.

It's often a logistical and diplomatic nightmare trying to convince the dwellers of a particular dimension to allow further access. That's even if they speak any language of earth, or even breathe oxygen. For example, there are very few tourists to the methane and sulphur rich dimension referred to as universe D-474. Despite boasting the most impressive sunsets of any other world and a colour spectrum nine times as complex as our universe, the smell is quite unbearable.

I'm tired now, that will have to do. I'm pretty sure I nailed it anyway. I'll ask her out tomorrow. Anyway, the trickiest part is already finished. We've located the dimension containing Heaven. Now all we have to do is drill inside.

* * *

"Can I get you anything for the headache my Lord?" The angel Simiel waved and spoke loudly. God was wearing noise cancelling headphones and couldn't hear him. He busied himself tidying up, content in his own company.

For centuries it usually wasn't necessary for them to communicate in this way. But, ever since the whole Jesus thing, God had become intensely fascinated with humans and human things. Simiel understood why he had reconfigured all of paradise in a way that resembled and emulated earth in many of its physical attributes. He found it astonishingly beautiful in its creation. Think of earth without any of the minor annoyances like bad weather or wasps.

Admittedly not one of His best ideas. A bit like the lovely and much adored bee, but with no honey and it can stab you repeatedly if you annoy it. *Why did he create those again?* Simiel pondered. He wouldn't bother asking, God was already distracted as creatives often are. Heaven was now a lot like earth, but as God had imagined it at the start. Before He had lost the ability for further creation. Before His powers had come to an end.

Neither God nor Simiel were magical, divine or spiritual beings. God was an entity much like many others in the universe, albeit a unique one and by far the most powerful. *That I know of anyway.* Thought Simiel. The multiverse in all its complexity was infinite, no discernible beginning and no end. In one dimension within multitudes, existed this one. And, it was populated initially by an omnipotent, omnipresent and very lonely being.

God had created the dimension where humanity resided mainly out of boredom. It was also because his first creations, the angels like Simiel, were very poor conversationalists. Being made apart from him and not in his image like mankind was, they were a little on the subservient side. He had been too much of an idealist.

He had created beings that were too perfect and infallible. *Well, that is until one in particular of course went quite off script.* Simiel mused to himself. Humans challenged his decisions and questioned the natural order. It was refreshing! Angels just smiled and nodded most of the time. An entire universe full of yes-men. Simiel could understand why that would become exasperating, he just couldn't do anything about it. It's how he was made.

Simiel looked over God's shoulder at some of the various windows depicting human life. *What a condition.* He was both amazed and repulsed at the thought. Throughout the years of worship, soul searching and existential angst within his latest creations, for the life of him Simiel couldn't understand why the ones that kept the faith largely accepted the idea of an eternal and infinite God, but not an eternal and infinite universe. They'd feel much more relaxed about everything if they did. *There would be far less murdering and crusading and the like.* He shrugged, resuming his work.

The main problem was that for God, an eternity could pass like the blink of an eye. From the time it took for Him to create humankind, to the time it took for them to start blowing each other up with atom bombs, felt to Him like the time it might take for you or I to brew a pot of coffee. By the time he noticed what was going on it had all just got away from him a bit. Time was a troublesome thing, and even God had to play by its rules.

But now things were different. There had been a change. A unification among His creations. Humanity knew for certain there was a Heaven, and a God that resided there. Paradise was real, and His beloved children were drilling their way in with robots.

"No Simiel it's fine, it will pass, as all things do. Why don't you see if Lucy is hanging around anywhere, I have a favour to ask."

* * *

The energy inside the lab is electric. The entirety of the Eden Project facility is buzzing with whispers and rumours like a school playground. It seems rumours spread fast in a closed lab environment. I enjoy overhearing the conversations as I walk to my office. I clutch the soggy brown paper cup that contains my burnt coffee in one hand, and a display tablet in the other.

"I want to ask God about sickness, and death, what's all that about?"

"Is there really a plan to everything? Even my acne scars?"

"Wait, does that mean there's a Hell too?"

"I wonder if I'll get to see my wife again…"

"He's gonna get a piece of my mind, mark my words."

"What is *actually* the deal with wasps?"

The last one makes me look up from my computer. "Excuse me?" Ali frowns at me. She gets mad when I become so absorbed in the screen that I barely hear her.

"Wasps. Whats the deal with wasps? All they do is fly about and sting people." Ali has a charming British accent.

"Actually, a few species of wasps pollinate like bees do. Mostly they're predators, kind of like the insect version of a tiger, they control other pests and such. All part of the balance of nature." I respond in an almost automatic way. Her face says she's not satisfied.

"I still think they're pointless," she pouts, trailing off quietly. She caresses the jewelled stud on her silver nose ring as she often does when she was bored. I can't decide if I like nose rings or not. I go back to scanning the monitor in front of me back and forth. The live feed from the nanobots at universe D-0 is coming through clearly. Through a window displayed on screen, the pale distorted image of a vast city can vaguely be seen. The distortion comes from what the other scientists have come to refer to as The Pearly Gates.

It seems that universe D-0, referred to as Heaven by some of the younger and more excitable scientists, is behind some type of hardened, translucent wall. A vast bubble of the stuff exists around the contents of universe D-0 in its entirety, blocking off all access to what was inside. We've been alternating between diamond drilling and refined lasers. It seems to be doing the trick, but it's been slow going.

Science, while mostly exact, relies on the formulating and then subsequent proving of theories. Gravity for example, is simply a theory. The presence of gravitons has never been proven, and nobody has ever seen one. The theory that this is Heaven is based on a number of factors including data readings, and also visual appearance.

There are some shocking similarities between humanity's dimension and universe D-0. The nano-cameras have sent back imagery one might expect from a manmade concept of paradise. This theory is mainly accepted however due to the immense neon sign that had been up at the entrance to the place, which reads:

Welcome to Heaven.
Welcome to all God's children.

There is also footage of a slender and sheepish looking figure in white robes hurriedly switching the sign off in an effort to hide it. The man was wreathed in light which made him hard to make out, and interfered with the fragile camera lens.

"What do you want to ask God, Adam?" Ali is looking up from her work now, eyes fixed on me. Her gaze is heavier than before. I know I'll have to give a proper answer or I'll never hear the end of it.

"Why?"

"Why what?" Ali is obviously perplexed, "Why am I asking you that or what? Adam you're so irritating sometimes!" She's about to return to her work. I feel a mild panic.

"I want to ask him 'why?' That's all. Why all this? Why create life in the first place? Was it vanity? Does he feel the need to be worshipped and adored? Why even bother?" I find myself looking up at the ceiling as if I'm already talking to Him. Her expression is too intense for me. My questions came out like a child asking the same to their parent. It's embarrassing.

I glance at her during the awkward silence. Ali's mouth is hanging open slightly. She snaps herself out of a slight trance and points at me, eyebrows raised. "Good question!" For once she feels content by my answers. I know I can be maddeningly distant sometimes. Sometimes it's easier just to disconnect rather than feel everything all at once.

* * *

God watched the entire interaction play out on his LCD screen. He was sat back on a white leather lazy boy, with a large mug of oolong tea in one hand that He was sipping delicately. "Do you think anyone on earth knows how much you love neon signs?" Simiel asked.

"Probably not," He replied. "You know, those two would make a better couple than either of them will ever realise. He's too wrapped up in his work finding *me*, and she can't see past it! Children!" He chuckled.

God had said it many times. For humans, the entire point of their existence was merely to feel. Animals are a bit more specialist in their abilities. A practice run. To humans, he had given them the perfect balance of taste, touch, smell, hearing and sight. All for their enjoyment, and subsequently for his. Not only that, but he had provided a myriad of incredible things for them to experience with those five senses. There was even a sixth which they had yet to discover.

God was a voyeur. Think of it this way. If you watch a movie you absolutely love, there's only so many times you can rewatch it before it's not quite so interesting anymore. But, watching it with a friend for the first time? Now it's fresh again. Simiel always did enjoy their movie nights together. *Maybe we can watch The Empire Strikes Back again soon?* He could only hope.

It was a little sad to think of how it had been. For centuries God had been this way. Living vicariously through the lives of his creations. He had been omnipotent, omnipresent. He could be everywhere and feel everything there was to feel all at once. Every time one of his creations tasted something for the first time, he tasted it too. Every time they heard a song they loved and it moved them to tears, it moved him too. Whenever they fell in love, so did he. And he was addicted to it all.

This continued throughout the entirety of time. Right up until unknowingly, he had spent all of his energy. His lust for creation had been His undoing. He was like so many billions and trillions of lego blocks, pulling pieces out and putting them to use elsewhere. Now all he could do was watch. He could watch anything he liked, but that was it. No longer could he feel it. No longer could he truly experience it as they did. It truly irritated him at times.

"But *no*. All you want to do is think about the past! Think about the future! If you'd simply see what was right in front of your faces you'd *get it*." God continued, visibly frustrated. "I miss the good old days when people still made sacrifices to me. Remember? Burning bits of goat, tossing things they loved into the sea and all that." He sounded wistful. Simiel checked behind him over his shoulder before speaking up.

"My Lord, Lucifer is here to see you," he spoke in a hushed tone. He wasn't fearful, though he did find the angel of darkness made him very uncomfortable.

"Lucy! Good to see you, good to see you, how have you been?" God beamed a large smile, it created a light that would have instantly blinded any human standing in His presence. Lucifer made the shadows within the room appear larger. She appeared as a woman today, smoky and dark, but nondescript in terms of ethnicity. She could have been from almost anywhere. She was dressed comfortably in a fashionable deep purple tracksuit and expensive looking white leather running shoes.

Beelzebub, The Devil, Abaddon, Apollyon, Satan. She went by many names, but Lucy preferred what she called *the original*. It mean't morning-star after all, and who wouldn't want that? The thing about Lucifer, is that she never held even one percent of the almighty creator's power, but had exploited what little she had to the utmost. She was still free to roam between dimensions, and could be anywhere she chose in an instant. Possessions were a real thing, but it was more like hitching a ride on a meat wagon. Above all else however was her gift of speech. She was a remarkable temptress if the need arose, and could convince practically anyone of anything.

Human beings had never really been privy to the genuine interactions between God and The Devil. Most of their information was based off of hearsay from a few angels, lesser spirits, and certain men and women throughout history who had been "blessed" with visions. It's worth noting that a vision from God was simply an attempt by the almighty to download new information into a host brain to speed up humanity's development. This often didn't work out well, and could result in the subject losing their mind. That's why you see so many deranged people screaming on the bus in the evenings.

It was true that Lucifer had always been something of a black sheep among the angels. Lucifer was The Almighty's attempt at a slightly less subservient being, but the consequences were higher than anticipated. She had gotten above her station and suggested that she might be able to run the show better than God himself. What ensued was a scene akin to a parent spanking their child, and nothing more. To be honest after that, they got along rather well.

One of the most important elements of humanity was that they have free will. There genuinely was no *plan* for them as such, it was simply an ongoing experiment in sensation and interaction with the other people and universe around them. Lucifer became an integral part of all that. God allowed her down to the mortal realm every so often to help give people a nudge every now and then. She wasn't the source of evil or anything like that, although she did enjoy suggesting mischief now and then. No, when humans did terrible things, that was on them. It always had been.

"Lucy I want you to talk to Adam here. See if you can't get him to—"

"Give up this whole thing?" Lucy purred sweetly, "You know as well as I do he won't do that."

"I suppose not," God scratched his head. "Well, at least distract him a bit then will you? I just want this all to slow down."

"And why would I do that? I'm enjoying all this immensely. Seeing you pull your hair out is positively delightful. I feel indulgent just watching the whole thing. It's *delicious.*"

God knew she was just being her usual irritating self, but Lucy's reluctance to toy with a mortal meant only one thing. If the Devil didn't want to mess with a man, it was because the man couldn't be messed with. Nothing damaged Lucy's ego more than that. She found it infuriating.

"You're intolerable Lucy…you really always have been."

"You only have yourself to blame," she replied quickly. She never missed an opportunity to remind Him of that one.

"Oh just piss off then will you? I'm starting to get another headache because of that infernal drilling and your frankly *unbearable* voice." The Devil disappeared in a puff of deep purple smoke. God rolled His eyes, it was just so tacky.

* * *

The trill from a notification wakes me up from a nap. I've fallen asleep in front of my computer again. It's an email from Judie.

Hi Dr. Rizzo,
Thanks so much for your response to the interview questions. I'll get it to the editor for release in the next few days. And thanks for your offer of dinner.

I'm so sorry I didn't reply. I hope you understand, it would be unethical for a reporter to date a source.
Kind regards,
Judie.

No *x* this time, it was to be expected. *Why did you have to mention the methane dimension? You always mention the methane dimension.* Lara had told me in the past that I'm not good at reading cues. My phone vibrates with another notification. It's from Ali.

Do you like what you see? It reads. There's a picture attached. I yawn as I open it, still waking up. She is dressed in what appears to be nothing but an oversized t-shirt. It's emblazoned with the Eden Project logo, two fruit trees side by side. Her legs are bare all the way up to the top of the thigh and her body is contorted in such a way as to accentuate her figure dramatically. She is wearing a different nose piercing to the usual silver, embellished with a deep purple stone.

Is that new? I message back, referring to the nose ring. Ali replies quickly.

You mean these? In the next picture she has folded her arms low underneath her chest, giving the impression of a pushup bra. I slam the phone face down on the table. I'm suddenly very hot. It buzzes three more times before going silent. I don't know what's gotten into her but I need to finish what I'm doing and get to sleep. I grab a blueberry yoghurt from the refrigerator. Has the label always been such a deep shade of purple?

* * *

The following morning at work is a trial. Ali continuously attempts to pull my attention from work with every trick in the book. She drops things to pick them up in front of me, and asks me relentless questions about my dating history. Soon she begins the practice of standing unnecessarily close to me to converse about data and statistics. I feel drenched in her saccharine perfume and she's wearing a shorter skirt than usual. There are more undone buttons on her shirt than usual too. She's stuck to me like glue.

For a short while late in the morning, Ali leaves the room for a coffee. I stand up from my desk to escape, pocketing my portable work tablet and making for the exit. As I pull it open, she is on the other side, already walking in. She steps towards me with a seductive smirk on her face.

"I brought you your favourite, with a hint of something different." She says, handing me my usual black coffee, sprinkled in an odd manner with chocolate powder. The powder floating on top of the dark liquid looks vile and very out of place. I try a sip. *Gross.* She doesn't stop moving, backing me into the room with each deliberate step, edging closer.

I'm under slept, under caffeinated and just plain confused by Ali's sudden change in behaviour. "C-can you just b-back off for a minute please? Ali? Please?" I fix my eyes about one foot past her head to the left, palms up in a defensive posture. Her demeanour changes in an instant. As does her voice.

"You are so *boring* Adam. God *damn* it." The voice is no longer her own. It's an American accent that sounds somewhat refined. Quiet and well spoken. The voice speaks almost as if it's chewing on each word before spitting it out.

I reel backwards. All seduction is removed from her posture. I rub my eyes, blinking. Before me it's no longer my lab assistant. My vision blurs in and out, but I distinctly now see the form of a tall, powerfully built and graceful woman before me. She scratches the edge of her chin as if she has an invisible beard. The new woman takes a seat in the black wheeled chair by Ali's metal desk.

"W-who are you? Where's Ali?"

"You know, the first Adam I ever met was *far* more interesting. Definitely down for a good time. There aren't that many interesting Adams to be fair though. Adam West? First Batman, kind of cool. Adam Sandler, well, he's one of mine of course. Other than that, not many interesting Adams, no." She sits back in her chair and crosses one leg over the other, placing both of her hands delicately on one knee.

Comprehension crawls slowly through my

brain. It's like an army of marching ants that start their procession at the bottom of my face, moving it into position as they work their way to the top, raising my eyebrows as if mechanically.

"That's right honey. You're trying to wiggle your way into Heaven, so of course that means there must be a hell, and someone running the show down below, right?"

"Right."

"Wrong!" The woman speaks suddenly as if she has just figured the answer to some great question. She has an annoying cockiness about her.

"There's no hell…but you *are* the Devil…?"

"I prefer Lucifer. Friends call me Lucy." She leans forwards, extending her large palm towards me in a friendly gesture. I hesitate and stare at it blankly. "Oh don't worry this doesn't mean we're making a *deal* or anything so dreadfully cliché." She stretches it out further, giving my hand one firm shake. Hers feels like solid like twisted steel, but soft as if wrapped in new suede. I can't be sure if it's a hallucination due to lack of sleep, or if I can trust my own eyes. My hesitance and confusion is obviously humorous to the purple clad woman.

"Obviously no there's no hell. How could that make even the slightest bit of sense? What would the criteria be? You can search the Bible for it if you want. There's no mention of it there either." Her words seem to curl around the room along with the deep violet smoke emanating from somewhere on her person. "Are we going to throw Genghis Khan and Hitler into the same fiery pit as some non-believer? Some nobody who won't accept Jesus Christ as their lord and saviour because they're an *atheist?*" She hung on the last word like a child might do when teasing another.

"I suppose not."

"You suppose correct. All that stuff about fire and brimstone was a lot of scare tactics made up by the church. And as everyone knows, organised churches and religion are just scared little men trying to control other scared little men."   "That's true."

"It is. Not only that but historically, religion has always been man's favourite way to control their most prized possessions."

"Which are?"

"*Women*," she lets the word spill from her mouth like so much red wine from a glass.

"What do you mean possessions?"

"Oh come now little Adam."

"I don't follow."

"You see women as add-ons to your life. Accompaniments. Little side dishes to your grand story. Lara. Judie. Even pretty little Ali here," she rolls her hands down her hips mockingly.

"I suppose you're right there too."

"Of course I am. I'm *always* right. Look, if you must know, God made man and woman equally, yes. But man has come to dominate women through physicality, law making and just plain bullying. There's nothing God can do about it either. It would be an interference with the whole *free will* rule he's got such a hard-on for."

"There seems to be a lot of things he can't do anything about. Or won't."

"Oh believe me, he knows he's made mistakes."

"Look I've got a lot of work to do so…if that's all there is to it could you kindly leave my colleague and leave me to it?" I don't know if it's the absurdity of the situation or if I'm being emboldened by lack of sleep, but I begin to collect myself. Mirage or not, I still have so much to do.

"By all means, of course. To be honest this was just a bit of fun before things really change between you all and the big man upstairs. Personally I'd prefer you just keep on keeping on." Lucy is fiddling with various items on the desk in an absent minded fashion. She snaps several pencils in succession between her fingers, letting the tiny chips of wood and graphite fall where they may. She seems to like the anarchy of it. "I bet you have all kinds of questions for Him upstairs right? Why *good?* Why *evil?* Why *me?*"

"I suppose I do. But not really about good and evil. I think that's all relative to be honest. It all depends on who's writing the history books doesn't it?"

"Go on, enlighten me." Lucy changes her positioning, sitting herself on the floor cross legged in front of me. Her chin is resting on her hands and she smiles like a silly three year old. She has the appearance of a giant lavender spider, coiled up on the floor with her knees and elbows jutting out at angles.

"Well you mentioned Genghis Khan and Hitler right? To myself and this generation, most people will agree that what they did between them is altogether evil. Of course it is, from our perspective. But then Hitler and Genghis Khan didn't feel that way. What they were doing was really very *good* from their perspective." Lucy's gaze is unnerving.

"That's a bit of a grand example I suppose but you can look at it in smaller ways too. Maybe a young man who commits vandalism gets some sort of status boost among their peers for doing it. Maybe by doing that, he's protecting himself from being victimised by those around him in turn."

"But aren't some things inherently evil? Murder? Coveting thy neighbours wife?" Lucy smirks as the last word rolls off her tongue. It flicks almost reptile-like from her mouth occasionally.

"Well our society deems murder as evil, yes. But what about a teen girl murdering their abusive father to protect their mother from being strangled to death? Can you say thats an evil act? Is euthanasia of someone in extreme pain and suffering evil? Is it evil to put your dog down when they get an incurable and painful disease? Life isn't black and white. Life isn't good and evil. It is all completely relative to the people involved."

"And what if I were to murder you?" The Devil stood up in front of me. She was impressively tall and athletically built. Her long cruel-looking arms could probably do a lot of damage. *I need to start going to the gym.* She stands a head taller than me and casts a dark shadow over my face.

"Could you do something like that? Are you allowed?" I feel myself shrink slightly as she looms.

"Maybe I could? Maybe I never tried."

"Well, personally I don't want to be murdered. But I'm not sure I can weigh up the moral ramifications of that. A mortal man being murdered by the Devil seems like an evil thing on paper. Then again if the Devil is evil incarnate maybe it is? To be honest there's nothing remotely interesting to me about the moral side of it all. It's almost pointless wasting time trying to define anything like that."

"God you talk a lot." Lucy takes a step backwards, appearing to reduce in size. A warm smile crosses her face. "I'm not evil incarnate you know. And you're not a hypocrite, even in the face of your own death. No, I'm mainly just here to spin the wheel every so often. It's important to introduce a modicum of chaos now and then. You know Van Gogh?"

"The painter?"

"The very same. The whole 'giving your amputated ear to your prostitute lover' thing was my idea of course. But without the uncommon shifting in that mind, you'd never have *The Starry Night.* That's what it is to be a master at something, a creative. You have to be somewhat mad and self indulgent to have those ideas in the first place."

"So God is somewhat mad and self indulgent?"

My face suddenly flushes scarlet at the audacity of the question.

"You can ask Him yourself." Lucy's voice melts into that of Ali's again. My vision blurs. I blink what feels like purple smoke from my vision. It's my colleague in front of me again. Her eyes fall to her skimpy attire and widen in embarrassment.

"Adam! I'm, um… I'm sorry! I'm feeling sick. Can I take the afternoon off? I'll be back in tomorrow!" She scrambles to button her shirt and adjusts her skirt frantically.

"Of course, go, go. Hope you feel better." My head is spinning and I feel queasy. I sip the strange coffee again and resume analysis of the latest figures. We'll be through tomorrow. A new question for God burns in my mind.

* * *

The drills and lasers had done their work. Simiel watched the final cuts being made in The Pearly Gates. He made his way through the deserted streets of Heaven towards The House of God, high up a winding path at the top of a hill in the centre. He missed the other angels greatly, and also the souls that used to populate this vast idyllic metropolis.

Heaven was asymmetrical in every way. Buildings flowed in between and around fixtures like waterfalls and forests as naturally as the many winding streams and rivers that cut through it. You could walk for a day and never see the end of the city in one direction. Marble spire after marble spire, great palaces, gardens and parks as far as the eye could see. It was also a bit of a prison.

Over hundreds and thousands of years passed since the birth and death of the first humans. Throughout that time there had been many forms and incarnations of Heaven. The first was simply an endless well of energy and light. Your soul would be transmuted into the whole where you could experience the unending consciousness of the cosmos along with other human beings minds, souls and hearts all at once. It proved to be an issue of privacy for many so that idea was scrapped eventually.

God had also tried a Heaven whereby whoever arrived saw it in the way they had imagined it. If paradise to you was a gorgeous white marble city, that's what you'd see. If it was a vast and never ending tropical jungle paradise in your mind on earth, when you died that's where you were sent. For others, the afterlife was an eternal orgy of writhing flesh and naked bodies. For obvious reasons this model only lasted a few thousand years. It was far too complex to line up everyones fantasies.

Eventually God had settled on its current form, some time after Jesus' birth and death. In this familiar shape, the souls that ended up in Heaven were able to pick and choose for themselves how to spend eternity. However, even that had its limits. It was just so boring.

Simiel had to admit, he was jealous of God's final creations. He had made man's mind especially for the physical earth. Humans were made in His image but with all the complexity of Gods themselves. They just didn't have the overt and somewhat dangerous powers that came with the territory. The purpose of a human was to be, in a very physical sense. When given the option of an endless paradise, even that became boring after a while, there was no conflict. No reason for growth. It was just a hedonistic mess of existence without purpose.

The angel looked longingly at the rows of empty houses he passed by. *It's such a shame that it all had to stop. He never knew when enough was enough.* There was no Hell, but God did have to make yet another separate location for all those undesirables who just simply weren't interested in peace and harmony. That's how humans are, they make up their own mind.

Eventually He started to notice some more problems. There were many people in Heaven with loved ones in this other place. It was impossible for them to have eternity in happiness with their lovers, friends, fathers, brothers, mothers, children and other family members or loved ones away from them. God really hadn't thought this one through.

Over time more and more people decided to stay with their loved ones out of Heaven. They would rather eternity as neighbours to Himmler, Ted

Bundy and Walt Disney (you can only orphan so many of your beloved fictional characters before people realise there's something seriously wrong with you), than to be without those that had been so close to them during their lives.

So God emptied both paradise and the other place, and gave the souls leave to travel where they would throughout the multiverse, human and angel alike. *Gabriel was such a good conversationalist. Michael not so much.* Simiel reminisced. Some found their way back to each other and remained as pure energy, travelling the infinite cosmos as lovers for the rest of time. Other souls returned to earth and humanity, inhabiting newly forming cells as they were conceived by their parents to be reborn for a fresh chance at life.

This suited God too. Human beings were always intended to be the experiment of feeling. If God *was* the universe, then so too were each of the creations made of him. Most human souls opted to return to human existence for more spins on the wheel of life. By allowing this, God was able to *feel* even more. Until he couldn't. Until all he could do was watch.

Simiel hurriedly walked through the great gates towards The House of God. He wasn't entirely sure what was about to happen. And, for one of the first times since time began, neither was God.

* * *

The sleek rubberised and reinforced metal mesh of my gate suit feels stifling. I'm a lab man, not an adventurer. However, this being the greatest discovery of the century behind the multiverse itself, I'm expected to head the expedition into universe D-0. *Not my idea of a good time.* I would much rather have watched it all on my screen in the office. Better yet, at home. I wonder if God is watching too somehow. I check my phone one last time. No response from Ali. I seal my helmet with four clicks around the base and step into the transport tube.

Behind me sit three others. It's a small team, and the choices for who made the cut fascinate me. One of them is of course the most pre-eminent engineer the project could find. She asked that everyone simply call her Watts. She's a gruff and practical older woman, with seemingly no set of beliefs to call her own other than to keep her head down, work hard, and rest harder after. She has no interest whatsoever in whatever being lay on the other side, she's just there to get us across and back in one piece. I like her.

The other two are more unusual choices. Seated directly behind me is a doctor of philosophical studies, John Pep. In fact not only that, but he's the world's most famous author on the subject. Apparently being called Dr. Pep is a powerful unique selling point for his books. He's considered to be an expert in all things faith and religion. It's generally assumed he'll have better questions for whatever God or gods lay on the other side of the gate.

Lastly, seated at the back of the molecular transport tube capsule is a six year old child. A girl with chocolate coloured hair. Dr. Pep's daughter, Laura. The choice to bring her, along with the subsequent legal storm for bringing a child on a scientific expedition, was made by John himself.

"The Bible states quite clearly, 'Truly I tell you, unless you change and become like little children, you will never enter the kingdom of Heaven'. Matthew eighteen verse three. And I'll tell you something else, that's good enough for me to want to bring her along." John hailed from Texas. His southern drawl is comforting to listen to.

Slowly, the molecular rearrangement system (MRS), and high powered particle cannon fire up with a great whirring and the sounds of crackling electricity. The room surrounding the transportation vessel glows blue. The process used for reducing the size of the transport to that of a single atom is extremely disorienting and I'm already feeling nauseous.

It's essentially an extreme process of *folding*. It has long been held that potentially enormous amounts of information, and even entire universes could be contained within the walls of a particle such as a proton or electron. It was this theory that led to the compression transportation technology humanity now relied on for multiverse travel. The MRS folds matter inside it, again and again, until it's no more than information. It isn't my first time, but trying to articulate the actual experience is nearly impossible.

Imagine perhaps the process of being born. Everything that you are or will be, is contained within the walls of a great stomach. You are surrounded by a warm and dim crimson light. Muffled and distant sounds from the outside you can't identify reach your ears. You are surrounded and compressed tight on all sides. You feel secure. There is the sudden pressure of muscular contractions, spasming and pushing you down towards the birth canal. What starts next is a relentless spiralling feeling as you corkscrew downwards, your softened head being squashed to fit through the exit that has been prepared for you. Soon after, your eyes are hit with bright light. You take your first ever breath and look around at your surroundings, kicking and screaming and with absolutely no comprehension of what you are now seeing. If you can picture that, you are about one-tenth of the way to understanding what it's like to have your body and mind compressed into mere information, and then shot out of a molecular cannon into another dimension.

On the other side of the gate we endure the customary dizziness and occasional bout of vomiting for the next twenty minutes. Watts takes the lead and strides first through the gap in The Pearly Gates. They are several metres thick and translucent all the way through to the other side. Their material is like nothing any of us has ever seen before. Incredibly hard and smooth as marble, cool to the touch as I run my hand along it.

The sprawling and empty cityscape comes into view. Watts' mouth opens in shock, "Well would you look at that. It'd take quite a team of people to throw all this together. There's no end to it!" she posited, admiring the splendour of the craftsmanship in each unique structure and building.

"Or, just one." A man appears from behind the corner of a walled garden, adorned with vines and wreathed all over with flowers none of us can identify. He stands at an average height, but is very handsome and physically well built. He's dressed simply in soft white robes. Behind him burns the apparition of what appears to be two wings, but they give more the appearance of huge blades of light behind him. I can't look at them directly for too long.

"I'm g-guessing you're an…an," Dr. Pep stammers uncontrollably.

"An angel! You're an *angel,*" squeaks Laura excitedly.

"My name is Simiel. Will you all come with me? It's a long walk to His house," Simiel gestures behind him down the road. Slack jawed, we oblige and follow the man.

Simiel is happy to answer some of our questions as we go. As we make the walk to The House of God, we discover why Heaven is now empty, and more about the history of the angels. None of it seems to make a lot of sense. The impression I get is that God simply does things, and deals with the fallout afterwards. It was something between science and art. I can't put my finger on it but according to the rhetoric we should be grateful regardless.

Soon we arrive. The entire generous portion of land both outside and inside the main door is absolutely littered with all sorts of bizarre objects, antiques, relics and junk. Mainly junk.

"Ah yes. He's something of a collector. He adores the creations of his creations," Simiel explains. I glance over at the corner of the main welcoming hall, strewn with all manner of musical instruments. Alongside that is a heap of vinyl records and record players, followed by an unbelievably large selection of variously sized hats.

Through the lobby area, Simiel leads us to a huge winding staircase which is again, very cluttered. It's covered with statues of bronze, marble and other types of stone in haphazard order. At the top, it opens out into an enormous hall with a balcony at the far end. Sitting in a white lazy boy chair, in front of the balcony with the windows open behind Him, sits a figure. My legs weaken inexplicably. I step forward cautiously and follow the angel.

Simiel had referred to God as a Him, but now standing in his presence this made absolutely no sense. His appearance is that of a man one-second, a woman the next. He is both fatherly and motherly all at once. I tried to wrap my head around it. If all human life flowed from a mother, then surely the creator of the universe could potentially be female. Except he isn't...or she isn't, or is. It's confusing to look upon and fathom. Whatever gender the being is, their skin is a blended and somewhat golden olive tone. Or is it something else? It changes. The features constantly shift too and are nondescript, except for long and beautiful flowing white hair, and a pair of piercing and dark eyes that seem themselves to reflect stars that are not even out at this time of the day. Fixing my eyes on God is demanding. He speaks.

"Adam, well-done. You made it. You've come home." The voice is grand, complex. Maybe a little rehearsed even. It sounds sure of itself, but overly practiced. "Come, what do you want to ask of me. Speak! You may ask anything you wish." Dr. Pep speaks first, pushing his way past me.

"What is the meaning of life?" He blurts out. It's clumsy, and must have sounded better in his head. God smiles and I can swear the room gets brighter.

"Nothing," says God.

"Nothing?"

"Everything," continues God.

"That doesn't make any sense!" Laura pipes up from behind us. Honestly I agreed with her, it feels like a cop out. Something a guru might say to his followers. God shifts his gaze towards the child.

"My child, it will. Tell me, what do you want to ask?" He smiles kindly, though I notice the left eye on his face twitch at the corner.

"Why did you make everything?" She walks forward a few paces, standing as tall as she can manage, bottom lip sticking out as she does so. I flash her an irritated look. That was my question.

"Would you really like to know?"

"Yes."

"Do you ever pick up a pen and paper, and just start drawing, just to see how the colours blend together?"

"Well, yeah." Laura looks puzzled. We all are.

"So do I." He gives another kind smile, the kind your grandpa gives you as he slips you a dollar at Christmas time. It looks forced, like he's trying to sound wise. I'm reaching the limits of my patience. I speak up.

"So what you're saying is, and please correct me if I'm wrong, that you made everyone and everything out of boredom?" I'm struggling to keep my composure, I can feel my voice shaking slightly.

"Well, no, uh," God clears his throat and regains himself. "Of course, I can explain. What would you like to know?" He's faltering. I feel like he's been dreading this moment.

"Do you realise the pain, and the horror that goes on every day back on earth? The unimaginable suffering you have caused with your shoddy workmanship?"

My voice is raised now uncontrollably. "You're

just some irresponsible alien being! One with too much power. And my guess is that power has run out, why else would you *still* be here? Why haven't you struck me down yet? Why didn't you stop me from coming here? It's because you *couldn't*, could you? You started this whole ride spinning and now you can't stop it! What kind of egotistical insanity would lead anyone to have the *hubris* to do what you have done? You can't even answer that, can you?"

Years of frustration and pain wells up inside me as I continue my tirade against God. I take a step forward towards the chair with each new point I make. I feel as if I'm standing outside of my own body. It's arrogant but who cares? God *gave* us this egotism. Just like him. I feel as if all of humanity is speaking through me in that moment. No questions, no pleases or thank yous. It's just blind anger and rage and torment all coming out at once. It feels good, it feels cathartic. It feels human.

God stands from his lazy boy to speak. "I made you to *love* my child, to love and be loved. If only you—." I swing my closed fist as hard as I can straight into the nose of the almighty creator before me. My hand explodes in pain. I've never hit anyone in my life. *I think I've broken it.*

Father, son, holy spirit. It's all one and the same. God had made himself into a being of flesh and blood so that he could enjoy the human experience, now he's getting the full deal. His introduction to actual pain is a harsh one. He crashes backwards into his cushioned chair and clutches his face in disbelief. I turn my back and storm towards the exit, ignoring the pleas and admonishments from Simiel and the others.

"What will you do here, now that you know?" God's voice squeaks through his broken nose. "What will become of Heaven now that you've found it?" I stop in my tracks.

"Tourism, probably." I shrug. It will be the same thing humans do with everything they discover. Every tropical island get's a McDonalds, every animal becomes a stuffed toy plushie as it is hounded to extinction. Heaven will be no different. It will simply become an attraction. God will fall victim to the insatiable hunger to consume that he has built so lovingly by happy accident into his creations, hundreds and thousands of years prior.

"Although," I continue. "I did have one more question for you." I turn and stand at the top of the stairs, backlit by an immense skylight above and behind me. I am the silhouette of every human all at once as I open my mouth to speak.

ABOUT THE AUTHOR

Born in 1989 in London, England, to an American mother and English father. Aaron originally worked in sales and marketing for a decade whilst pursuing a career as a competitive athlete. Later he moved full time into life as a martial arts and personal performance coach. He currently juggles his time between fatherhood, writing, teaching, and mental coaching, and is an avid consumer of baked goods.

This is the first collection of his written work, started after the birth of his daughter and completed during the global quarantine of 2020.

You can find out more about Aaron at his website, www.frameworkmind.com.

Printed in Great Britain
by Amazon